Brian could still remember how it had felt to hold her on the riverbank and think about what it would have felt like to lose her.

He thought of how selfish he'd been to ask Shelly to come with him on this trip and get her involved in this whole ugly scene.

He thought of how unfair he'd been to her.

He wondered how all the feelings he'd ever had for her, the ones he'd taken for granted, that he'd never given a second thought to, could have gotten this tangled up inside him at this moment. And God help him, he couldn't help but think of all the things he'd done to her in his mind, in that incredible dream, and he wondered how many of them had been real.

How many of them could have been real without him realizing it?

Dear Reader,

This month it's my pleasure to bring you one of the most-requested books we've ever published: *Loving Evangeline* by Linda Howard. This story features Robert Cannon, first seen in her tremendously popular *Duncan's Bride,* and in Evangeline Shaw he meets a woman who is his perfect match—and then some! Don't miss it!

Don't miss the rest of this month's books, either, or you'll end up regretting it. We've also got *A Very Convenient Marriage* by Dallas Schulze, and the next in Marilyn Pappano's "Southern Knights" miniseries, *Regarding Remy.* And then there's *Surrogate Dad* by Marion Smith Collins, as well as *Not His Wife* by Sally Tyler Hayes and *Georgia on My Mind* by Clara Wimberly. In short, a stellar lineup by some of the best authors going, and they're all yours—courtesy of Silhouette Intimate Moments.

Enjoy!

Leslie Wainger
Senior Editor and Editorial Coordinator

Please address questions and book requests to:
Silhouette Reader Service
U.S.: 3010 Walden Ave., P.O. Box 1325, Buffalo, NY 14269
Canadian: P.O. Box 609, Fort Erie, Ont. L2A 5X3

NOT HIS WIFE

SALLY TYLER HAYES

Silhouette®

INTIMATE™ MOMENTS®

Published by Silhouette Books

America's Publisher of Contemporary Romance

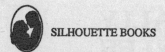 SILHOUETTE BOOKS

ISBN 0-373-07611-8

NOT HIS WIFE

Copyright © 1994 by Teresa Hill

This edition published by arrangement with Harlequin Enterprises B.V.

® and TM are trademarks of Harlequin Enterprises B.V., used under license. Trademarks indicated with ® are registered in the United States Patent and Trademark Office, the Canadian Trade Marks Office and in other countries.

Printed in U.S.A.

Books by Sally Tyler Hayes

Silhouette Intimate Moments

Whose Child Is This? #439
Dixon's Bluff #485
Days Gone By #549
Not His Wife #611

SALLY TYLER HAYES

lives by the ocean—a long-held dream of hers—with her husband, her young son and new baby daughter. A journalist for a newspaper in her home state of South Carolina, she fondly remembers that her decision to write and explore the frontiers of romance came at about the same time she discovered, in junior high, that she'd never be able to join the crew of the *Starship Enterprise*.

Busy with a full-time job and a full-time family, she confesses that she writes during her children's nap time and after they go to bed at night.

To Christina,

Despite the fact that her house is spotless,
her hair curled, her face perfectly made-up.
I can even overlook the size-five jeans.

And to Paula,

Because, like me, her house isn't spotless,
her hair isn't curled and her face seldom made-up.
Because only in her dreams could she wear size-five
jeans and because my baby girl loves her almost as
much as she loves me.

This is for the day getting the book out
on time became a group project
and for the day I realized I was so lucky
to have you two as friends.

Prologue

It came in February, tucked so innocently between a Christmas-laden charge-card bill and an offer for a totally free surprise gift valued at no less than one hundred dollars.

The letter that caught her attention was in an envelope made of the finest cream-colored stationery. It bore a Tallahassee postmark and an address she recognized; it was right next door to the place where she'd grown up.

Call it intuition, call it a sixth sense, but Shelly Wilkerson knew she didn't want to open that envelope.

She set her briefcase and her carton of curry chicken and rice down on the counter, then threw the rest of the mail aside. Feeling more than a little shaky, she pulled out a stool and sat down, all the while calling herself ten different kinds of a fool.

She was almost positive she knew what was in the envelope. She'd believed this was coming forever, had known for certain for almost a year. So it was no surprise.

She'd wanted this to happen. She'd waited for it—for all her foolish dreams to come crashing down around her, as she'd always known they would.

Still, there were little butterflies flying around frantically in her stomach when she pulled the letter opener out of a drawer and slit the envelope open in a single, trembling stroke.

She felt absolutely sick inside when she saw the telltale inner envelope of the same heavy cotton paper, then her name in that familiar, graceful script she recognized immediately as Rebecca's mother's. She didn't need to open the inner envelope to know what was inside.

Brian Sandelle and Rebecca Harwell, two of her dearest childhood friends, were finally getting married.

Shelly swallowed hard and let the envelope drop to the counter.

She had no right to react that way, she told herself. She wasn't a little girl anymore. She was a woman, and a woman couldn't live her whole life on sweet dreams of a tall, dark-eyed man and all the possibilities of what might have been.

It was time she set those dreams aside and stopped comparing every man she met to the one so firmly entrenched in her heart. It was time to move on, to start over, to fill that gaping hole this man left in her heart.

Shelly ended up leaving the food sitting on the counter. She'd lost her appetite.

And she never bothered to read the wedding invitation.

Chapter 1

Four weeks later

The phone rang, sounding absurdly loud in the deserted engineering office, and startled Shelly Wilkerson.

It wasn't quite six on a Monday morning. Normally she wouldn't be caught dead at the office at this hour—because a certain man she knew, one she'd vowed to avoid at any cost, liked to come to work early, as well.

Unfortunately the engineering firm was putting together a bid for some work on a huge new condominium complex, and Shelly was the engineer on staff who coordinated all the details. The electrical engineer on staff had let her down on this project. He'd been slow in finishing with his part of the construction plans, and this had put her behind schedule.

So here she was, coming in at dawn, trying to catch up to meet the bid deadline, and one thing she hadn't counted on was having to contend with the phone. She wondered who in the world would call a business at this hour. It had to be a wrong number, she decided as she picked up the phone.

"Williams Engineering," she said.

"Shelly?" The man's voice was muffled and strangely void of any inflection.

"Yes," she said, wondering how he knew who she was.

"You've got to get out of there, Shelly. It's not safe for you to work there anymore."

"What?" she said, whirling around from one side to the other, looking out over the mostly darkened office, her vision all but blocked by the shoulder-high partitions that separated the employee work stations.

Was he watching her now? Right this minute? Who was he? How did he know her? How did he know she was at work at this hour?

"The firm," the man said. "There are things you don't know about, things you don't understand, and you need to get out of there now."

She was still turning from side to side, watching her back, feeling as if someone were watching her. Someone must have been watching her.

"Who is this?" she demanded to know. Despite the fact that she couldn't place the voice, there was something vaguely familiar about it.

"A friend," the man said. "One who's worried about you."

"I don't know what you're talking about, but—"

"I can't explain. I've already told you more than I should. And for God's sake, don't tell anyone about this call. Just get out of that office before it all hits the fan."

"Wait a minute," Shelly said. "Do I know you?"

But it was too late. The phone clicked in her ear as the line went dead.

She hung up the receiver, and in the next instant she heard a door closing in the front of the office. Shelly clamped a hand over her mouth, afraid that some sound would escape her and lead the person right to her.

Who could it be? Who was that man on the phone? He said he was a friend, and although his words had frightened her he hadn't said anything in a threatening way. He seemed very serious, very deliberate and quite calm about the whole thing.

The sound of footsteps came to her. There was someone moving through the office.

Danger, the man on the phone had said. Here? She'd worked here for four years, ever since she graduated from engineering school.

The owner, Charlie Williams, was more of a father figure to her than a boss, and she counted everyone who worked at the small firm among her friends.

But... The footsteps were coming closer. Shelly just sat there, shaking in her shoes, wondering where she could hide and what she might be able to use to defend herself.

She didn't have an office, actually, more like a cubicle with shoulder-high dividers that broke up the big, open room. Unfortunately her cubicle was in the middle of the room.

There was only one way out—the way the intruder had come in. There was an emergency exit and a fire escape at the other end of the room, but she didn't think she could make it down the central hallway without the intruder seeing her.

Danger, the man on the phone had said. What kind of danger? Footsteps coming closer with every passing minute. What was she going to do?

And then the footsteps were right behind her.

Shelly realized that she'd waited too long to simply call 911. She picked up a big crystal paperweight off her desk— the hardest thing within reach—and lifted it over her head

as she stood and whirled around, finding a man right behind her.

"Ahh," she screamed as she nearly dropped the paperweight on him.

"Shelly?" said the man—a dangerous man—the most
dangerous man she knew. "Hey, what's this?"

Oh, yes, it did get more and more dangerous at this office, every day she stayed, every day since he'd come to work
here—though she knew that wasn't the danger her mysterious caller had referred to.

No one knew how dangerous this man was to her, and she
intended to keep it that way.

"Brian," she said, relieved that she no longer had to
worry about an intruder, yet dismayed to find she'd been
right in assuming that coming to the office this early would
put her into close contact with him. "You scared me."

"I guess so," he said. He'd caught the paperweight when
she would have dropped it and set it down on her desk. Then
he took her by the arms. "You're trembling."

Oh, yes. She was trembling harder than she had been before, now that he held her loosely in his arms.

He was the reason she never came to work this early anymore.

"What's wrong?" he asked, still holding her, slipping so
easily into that never forgotten role as her protector.

"Nothing." She shrugged easily, shook off his hold and
sat down in her chair, hoping to put some distance between
them.

She thought wrong. He pushed her stack of manila fold-
ers aside and sat down on the edge of the desk.

"You'd crack this rock over my head for nothing,
squirt?"

That silly childhood nickname made her stand up faster than anything else he could have said to her, and he knew it, too. "I will if you keep calling me that."

"Guess it doesn't do much for your professional image," he said, smiling easily.

"No, it doesn't," she said, her heartbeat racing.

She'd known him forever, it seemed. She'd thought he was something to look at when he was in college. She hadn't seen him more than a half-dozen times since then, until he'd come to work here last spring. So she hadn't been prepared for what had happened to him through the years. He was thirty-one now, and the years had been kind to him. He was taller, broader through the chest, stronger, even more solid than before.

That's how she always thought of him—rock solid, for his physical strength and his dependability, his loyalty, his honesty, his determination.

He was the kind of man a woman could count on, no matter what kind of trouble came her way, and Brian had always looked out for her.

Only problem was, he'd never grown to love her the way she loved him.

"So." He leaned forward on the desk, coming even closer now. "You going to tell me what's wrong?"

And while he might not know all her secrets, he knew her too well.

"It was nothing," she said, dropping her eyes, refusing to let herself look at him because she was afraid he'd see something in her eyes that he shouldn't. "I didn't hear your keys in the lock. I just heard someone walking around in the office and I thought someone had broken in."

She had no intention of telling him about the strange phone call. She'd never get out of his sight if she did.

Sometimes—no, most of the time—Brian Sandelle had trouble remembering that she wasn't a little girl anymore. And given the slightest reason, he could become incredibly protective of her.

She couldn't stand to have him hovering around her.

Besides—danger in this office? She just shook her head at the thought. It had to be some silly prank. The greatest danger to her in this office was standing right in front of her.

"Want some coffee?" she asked, knowing of his weakness for caffeine and ready to exploit it. "I started a pot a few minutes ago. It should be done by now."

He gave her a look that told her he wasn't ready to drop this, but took her hand and pulled her up from the chair, anyway, the promise of caffeine winning out.

They headed for the small kitchenette the engineering firm shared with the accounting office next door, and along the way, Shelly managed to pull her hand from his.

"So what are you doing this weekend?" he asked as he held an empty coffee mug under the still-dripping spout while she poured a cup for each of them from the half-full pot.

He hadn't been willing to wait for it to finish brewing. Besides, they both liked their coffee strong.

"I don't know," she said, pushing the pot back under the dripping stream of liquid as he pulled the mug away, spilling only a little of the coffee dripping from the spout. It hissed and danced along the burner, and she watched it, mesmerized for a moment. This was how it felt, she decided. If her skin could talk, this is what it would say when he touched her.

Shelly handed him his coffee and tried to remember what they'd been talking about.

The weekend. Surely they could have a safe conversation about that.

"I hadn't thought about it," she said. "What's the weather supposed to be like?"

"Rain," he said. "Saturday and Sunday."

She made a face and sipped her coffee.

Brian laughed. "I had an idea. Why don't you let me take you away from all this? Let's get out of town for the weekend."

Shelly nearly choked, then found herself afraid to meet his eyes as the heat flooded her cheeks.

It wasn't what she thought. She was certain of that. She'd known the man since she was six, for God's sake.

What in the world was going on this morning?

Shelly just stared at him, her mouth hanging open until she finally remembered to close it.

And for a minute, the only thing she could think about was the way she'd always known that one day she was going to totally humiliate herself in front of this man. Maybe that day had finally come.

A clattering sound brought her back to the problem at hand. It was noise her cup made as it bounced off the hard tile floor and broke into pieces.

She'd dropped her coffee. She felt the wetness on her arm before she felt the pain.

"Ouch!" she said when she finally realized the coffee was burning through the sleeve of her cotton blouse. She shook her head in amazement at what she'd done.

Less than five minutes alone with the man, and he'd reduced her to this.

"Here, let me help." Brian was beside her, checking her hand, unbuttoning the cuff of her sleeve, grinning at her. "I guess some things never change, Shel."

"No," she said softly, eating him up with her eyes at the same time she took a little step away from him. "Some things never change."

He was tall enough to tower over her, broad through the shoulder, lean through the hips, with that short-cropped, thick brown hair and those eyes—the darkest eyes she'd ever seen. She could get so lost in them she'd forget her own name.

And—as the wetness on her forearm reminded her—he shook her up so badly she turned into a klutz whenever she got within ten feet of him. She always had, probably always would.

Of course, he didn't know that. He thought she was this clumsy around everyone.

Brian finished rolling up her sleeve. For the second time, Shelly stepped back, this time as far away from him as the confined space of the office kitchenette would allow.

She had to be so careful around him, because she had trouble hiding her reaction to him. And the worst thing she could imagine would be having him realize how she felt about him.

"Hang on," he said. She could breathe again as he turned back to the cabinet drawers, searching through them until he found a dishrag.

He ran cold water over it, then turned back to her.

"Here," he said, taking her hand in one of his and putting the cool cloth over the burn.

"Better?" he asked.

"Yes." It was all she could manage, so she just stood there in the little kitchen, much too close to the tall, lean, rock-solid man, and wondered what it would take to drive him out of her heart forever.

She'd hoped that marriage would do it—his marriage to someone else, that is. Judging from the invitation she'd received in February, she didn't have long to wait for that to happen.

And she looked forward to that day. It was going to be the day she shut him out of her heart forever.

Because it was hopeless to go on loving him. She knew that in her mind, denied it in her heart.

"Here," he said after he'd found some ice cubes in the small refrigerator. "Let's see if this helps."

Shelly took a deep, hopefully steadying breath—a definite mistake. She simply drew in the all-too-familiar scent of him—something warm and musky, thoroughly unsettling despite the familiarity of it.

She looked down at the hands that held her injured arm. She knew those hands so well, knew their strong yet gentle touch, knew just as certainly that they would never touch her in quite the same way they touched the woman he loved.

"Better?" he asked again, his dark eyes locking on hers.

"A little," she lied absently, her mind lost in their tangled past.

"I didn't mean to startle you," he said.

She laughed, the sound tinged with desperation.

"I'm not sure how your fiancée would feel about that— you going away for the weekend with another woman," she said with a forced smile and a laugh as she tried to make a joke of it.

It had to be nearly time for his wedding, she thought. He mentioned a few things about his and Rebecca's plans to Shelly months ago, but hadn't said much lately.

She'd gotten better at avoiding him after work or sticking to business topics while they had to be together at the office.

She didn't think she could stand to listen to him telling her about his wedding plans.

And, like a coward, she'd left the unopened invitation in the wicker basket where she kept her mail, as if she could ignore the whole thing and make it go away.

It seemed she wasn't as eager as she thought for him to finally marry.

"Well." She forced herself to go on, avoiding his eyes, trying for all she was worth to hide her feelings from him. "You're not getting cold feet, are you?"

It was a ludicrous idea, actually. Brian wasn't afraid of anything. He was a very careful, methodical man. He thought things through to the end, made his decisions and stuck to them.

He would have—

She paused in her thoughts as the part of her brain that always zeroed in on him took note of the fact that he'd gone unnaturally still and silent beside her. Shelly made herself look at him then. Someone who didn't know him as well as she did probably wouldn't even have noticed, but she did.

There was a bleakness to his expression, a guarded look to his dark brown eyes, a smile that wasn't really a smile on his lips.

Brian squeezed her hand once, then put her own hand over the ice-filled cloth he was holding over her burn. He turned and headed toward the door, then turned back to her when he reached the doorway.

She closed her eyes and listened to the eerie quiet of the early morning hours in the empty office. The coffee was still gurgling and spitting and hissing.

The office outside was still dark and silent, probably would be for another two hours. It was Shelly's favorite time to work without interruptions.

It had been a shock to find him here one morning during that first week he'd come to work there. She'd spent at least six years trying to get him to notice her and another six trying to get him out of her heart.

Neither effort had succeeded, although she had been able to deal with it in the time she hadn't been living practically in his backyard.

Until he'd started working here, she'd only seen him three times in the past six years, the last time was when her father died.

It had been sudden—his heart—and he'd died before he fell to the ground. Brian had come to get her at college. Her father was the only relative she had left, and Brian hadn't wanted her to be alone when she found out he was gone.

It had been his shoulder she'd cried upon when he told her as gently as he could what had happened, his hand that she'd grabbed on to during the funeral, his arms that had locked around her and gently but firmly led her away from the grave site.

He did care about her, and, in his own way, he probably loved her. But not the way she wanted to be loved.

Certainly not in the way a man loves a woman he takes away for the weekend.

"What is it, Brian?" she asked when she couldn't stand it anymore.

He just blurted it out then. "Rebecca and I aren't getting married."

"What?" Shelly forgot all about the burn on her arm.

He loved Rebecca. He'd always loved her, and Shelly believed Rebecca loved him, as well.

It was simply the way of the world, like some cosmic force. There were laws about these things, and they couldn't be broken.

Brian loved Rebecca. She loved him back. In the end, they would be together, and Shelly would have to find a way to live without him.

He and Rebecca had been engaged when he'd moved here. Shelly had actually helped him start house hunting while he waited for Rebecca to close her business in Tallahassee, pack up her things and her little boy's and join him in Naples.

What in the world had happened?

She didn't ask him, because she knew she didn't have to. He'd tell her on his own, the way he'd always talked with her about him and Rebecca.

Now that Shelly thought about it, he'd probably been trying to tell her about it for some time now. But she'd pretended to be too busy, pretended to have other plans, anything to avoid being alone with him.

Brian shifted his weight from one foot to the other and leaned back against the doorway.

"Actually," he added, "what I said wasn't entirely correct. *I'm* not getting married. *Rebecca* is."

Shelly wondered if her mouth was hanging open again and decided that it probably was. Twice in the space of five minutes now, he'd left her speechless.

She couldn't say a word, just as she couldn't stop that small bit of hope that flared up inside her.

This man was going to be the death of her yet.

"Brian—" She forgot about the ice she'd been holding on her forearm, and it clattered to the floor amid the pieces of her shattered coffee cup.

Shelly closed her eyes and felt her cheeks burning once again. Damn the man, anyway. He'd done this to her ever since she hit puberty.

It was an effect much like the one that came from setting a magnet down next to a compass. Like that little arrow suspended on the dial, she just quivered in his presence, not knowing which end was up, her brain short-circuited by the power he had over her.

"Hey," Brian said, sneaking up on her while her mind wandered. His hand guided her chin up so he could see her face. "What's wrong with you?"

Every nerve ending in her body went haywire at the soft, sweet touch. She pulled away too quickly, drawing his attention even more than before with the sudden movement.

"Shelly?"

"I'm sorry," she said, suddenly finding herself ridiculously close to tears.

She wanted to hope. Despite everything, she wanted that desperately. She wanted to believe that she was going to get another chance with him.

Yet she couldn't do that. She'd done it too many times already. But she'd never really had a chance with him before, she argued with herself. She'd never stood a chance against Rebecca.

But if Rebecca was out of the picture...

"Let me get this cleaned up," she said. Afraid of the direction of her own thoughts, she decided she was better off concentrating on the bits of porcelain and ice and coffee that now littered the floor.

"I think it would be safer if I did it," Brian said, but she knelt on the floor to help him, anyway.

She managed to help clean up the mess without making any others. Then she got to her feet, avoiding his eyes at all cost as she backed away from him. She knew he was watching her closely, and she wondered what he saw when he looked at her. She prayed he didn't see a lovesick little girl who'd never gotten over her crush on him. She feared that was all he saw when he looked at her, even now when she was twenty-six years old.

"I guess this isn't your day," he said lightly.

She merely shook her head back and forth, feeling like a clumsy child who'd never measure up to the poised, elegant woman he'd always loved—the woman who was marrying another man. That was so hard to believe.

"Your arm okay?" he asked as they dumped the last of the ice in the sink.

She honestly hadn't felt a thing after the initial sting. She looked down at her arm, found the skin reddish, but couldn't tell if that was from the burn or the cold from the ice.

"I'm sorry—about you and Rebecca," she said.

He shrugged and glanced down the hallway again, empty no doubt. Why didn't someone else come to work?

"The wedding's this weekend in Tallahassee," Brian said. "I'm surprised you didn't get an invitation."

She barely stopped herself from telling him that she had—though it obviously wasn't the invitation to the wedding she'd anticipated. It was probably still in her mail basket. She hadn't even taken the necessary steps of declining the invitation and sending a gift. Rebecca's parents must think her incredibly rude.

"Anyway," Brian continued, "you haven't been home in ages...."

She hadn't, not since her father's death. There'd been nothing left for her in Tallahassee after that. No one but Brian, who'd never been hers in the first place.

"The whole town is going to be there," he said. "So you'd have a chance to catch up with some old friends, and my parents would love to see you."

"You want me to go to Rebecca's wedding with you?" she asked incredulously.

"I could use the company," he said.

She hesitated, knowing that the last thing in the world she needed was to spend the weekend with him, but not knowing how to tell him. She searched for something, some reason to refuse, to— "Wait a minute," she said. "Why would you want to go to Rebecca's wedding?"

"I have to, Shel. I need to watch her do it."

She nodded, understanding all too well. She'd planned to be in the church herself when Brian married Rebecca, although when the invitation had arrived she hadn't been able to find the courage to do what needed to be done.

What would some psychologist call it? Closure—that was it—a term that implied someone could tie up so much emotional baggage into a tidy little bundle and send it off into some black hole where it was never heard from again. If only it could be that easy.

"I don't know, Brian," she hedged, thinking of all that time she'd have to spend alone with him through the course of the weekend.

"Come on," he said. "Charlie would probably loan us the company plane. I could fly us up. We could be there in two and a half hours."

"I'm really swamped," she said. "That's the only reason I'm here so early this morning. We're so far behind on the condo project bid, and the whole thing is due—"

He silenced her quite effectively by using the fingertips of his right hand to tilt her chin up toward his face. He looked down into her eyes.

It was a light touch, a familiar one, next to nothing between good friends. She was sure he didn't think anything of touching her this way, but she did. Normally she wouldn't let herself be caught off guard and allow him to get this close.

"I don't want to go alone," he admitted quite seriously, then tried to make light of it. "Come on, Shelly. Isn't this the way women do it when they get dumped for someone else? Go to the wedding with the most gorgeous man they can find and try to convince everyone that they're having a wonderful time?''

Yes, she had to admit if she'd gone to his wedding there was no way she would have gone alone.

"Brian, it's not—"

"So I asked myself where I could find a wonderful woman who'd be interested in spending a weekend in Tallahassee, Florida, with me. And naturally I thought of you."

"Naturally." She tried to make light of it, but still felt her cheeks burn. "Brian—"

"Come on, Shel."

He could have coaxed her off a cliff with that tone of voice. And that's pretty much how she saw this trip—a leap off a very dangerous precipice. If she went, she'd spin all these impossible dreams in her head about him putting Rebecca out of his mind and finally turning to her. She'd already wasted so much time waiting for him. She felt old just thinking about it.

"Shelly?"

She made the mistake of looking at him again. She'd never been able to deny him anything. Only problem was, he'd asked so little of her. And then she started making deals with herself. She would go. She would give herself this time with him, a strange sort of goodbye, and she would let him show her that he still saw her as nothing more than a good friend. Then, with those feelings fresh in her memory, Shelly would finally move on with her life, without him.

"All right," she told him, deliberately not giving herself time to reconsider. "I'll go."

Chapter 2

Shelly hadn't been able to get out of the kitchen fast enough after her decision. Puzzled, Brian watched her go.

He wondered, once again, if he'd done something to offend her. For the life of him, he couldn't figure out what that might have been. They'd been friends forever. More than that, actually—he'd always thought of her as the sister he never had.

He could still remember the first time he saw her, a skinny little girl with skinned-up knees and big, sad eyes. She'd only been six years old, and she'd just lost her mother to cancer. He'd wanted very much to somehow make things better for her.

Her father was having trouble taking care of a little girl and working. The two of them came to live in what had once been the guesthouse on Brian's parents' ten-acre estate in Tallahassee. Shelly's father had become the grounds keeper.

Sometimes Shelly tagged along with her father while he worked. Sometimes she rattled around in the kitchen of

Brian's parents' home with the cook. But most of the time she'd been Brian's shadow. He'd been eleven when she'd come to live there, and it seemed she'd been a part of his life forever.

She'd left Tallahassee right after high school to attend college in North Carolina. Because of the scholarship, she'd claimed, but he'd always wondered what had happened to drive her away from the place that had been as much her home as his. She'd hardly ever come back to visit after that, and he'd never understood why.

Brian had been happy to find her here in Naples, working for an old friend of his father's. He'd looked forward to spending time with her again. He knew that since her father died several years ago, she was all alone in the world, and he hated thinking of her that way.

It was selfish of him to drag her off to this wedding this weekend, but she was one of the best friends he had in the world. He could tell her anything; it had always been like that between them. Brian didn't think he'd had any secrets from her when they'd been younger. She knew all about his relationship with Rebecca. If he was going to have anyone by his side this weekend, anyone who might understand, it was her.

He knew it was probably a mistake to go at all, but he had to go. If Rebecca Harwell was determined to go through with this marriage, she was going to have to walk past him on her way to the altar. He'd decided this morning that Rebecca was going to have to say her vows with him staring a hole in her back the entire time. Brian wouldn't make trouble at her wedding—he wasn't that kind of man—but he was going to be there.

He still couldn't believe Rebecca was going through with this. He'd been counting down the days, sure that something would happen before the wedding to show her what a mistake she was making. It wasn't that his ego was so big he couldn't imagine a woman preferring someone else over him. It was that he knew Rebecca. He could have swore that he knew her better than anyone, and that the two of them were meant to be together.

And now she was marrying another man.

He couldn't understand how he could have been so wrong about her. And he still worried that she was making a big mistake. So he was going to the wedding.

And once it was over, he was finally going to make himself forget about this woman he'd known his whole life, one he'd loved for nearly as long.

There were a dozen reasons why Shelly refused to let herself be hopeful, even now that she knew Rebecca intended to marry someone else. But the one that topped the list was the fact that she'd been through this all before. The sense of déjà vu was overwhelming.

Rebecca had been married years ago, briefly, while Brian was out of the country for a couple of years, working in the Peace Corps. It had been the only time in her life when Shelly had truly believed she was going to have a chance with Brian. She'd been in high school then, and she'd spun all these impossible dreams about what would happen when Brian returned. He'd find the woman he loved married to someone else, and for the first time he'd be free.

Shelly planned to be right there waiting for him.

Of course, it hadn't worked out that way. Rebecca's marriage hadn't lasted long, and Brian had been waiting to help her pick up the pieces.

That was when Shelly decided she couldn't stand it anymore. She'd left Tallahassee to go away to college because, as she saw it, putting some distance between her and Brian was the only hope she had of getting over him. She'd tried to find someone else, tried to find a fraction of the feelings she had for him with some other man. Trouble was, those other men just never measured up to Brian. She'd tried being friends with other men, dating them, even making love to them—except it had never felt like love.

It had never felt like what she felt for Brian.

Of course, that had been years ago, she argued with herself. She'd been more hopeful back then, more idealistic, more...immature. She'd still believed she could get most anything she wanted in life if only she worked hard enough and long enough.

She didn't believe that anymore.

And she'd been dealing with the whole thing better—at least she put him out of her mind on occasion. Until nearly a year ago when he'd ruined all her carefully laid plans by coming to work at the same engineering firm as she did.

She'd never imagined that the two of them would ever end up working together when she'd decided to enter engineering school. She didn't even want to do the same kind of work he did. But after a few advanced math classes in college, she'd been hooked.

In engineering, things made sense. If you put two and two together, you got four, every time. She liked the logic of it, the predictability. There'd been very little in her personal life that she could count on; she liked knowing that things made sense in her work at least. Of course, the work wasn't as logical or as predictable now that Brian was here.

It shouldn't have come as such a surprise to find him in Naples. When her boss, Charlie Williams, had lost a valued employee—a senior engineer who he relied upon to help him run the business—he'd needed help fast. He'd called his old friend and fellow engineer, Brian's father, to see if he could recommend someone to him.

As luck would have it, Brian had just decided that for the sake of his relationship with his father, it would be better if they gave up trying to work together. He'd come to Naples, and all Shelly's carefully won emotional distance from him had vanished into thin air.

She'd been fooling herself all along. She hadn't gotten over him. Maybe she never would.

She was at her apartment that night, sorting through her stack of bills, when she spotted the wedding invitation. And the fact that she hadn't given one thought all day to the man Rebecca *was* marrying spoke volumes about Shelly's mental state. She picked up the envelope and cautiously turned it over so the slit was facing upward. She still didn't want to open the blasted thing.

Why in the world would Rebecca marry anyone else? The town must be buzzing with speculation. Rebecca's family was every bit as wealthy and as well-known in Tallahassee society as the Sandelles were.

Shelly didn't doubt that, even though she'd severed all ties with the area after her father died, there were a half-dozen people she could call and get all the details.

Yet she hesitated to do that.

She hadn't even been able to bring herself to the point of opening the invitation and finding out the name of the groom. She felt as if she were about to commit some horrible invasion of Brian's privacy, though obviously that had already been done when Rebecca's wedding invitations had gone out. The wedding ceremony would make it as public as it possibly could be.

It would have helped if, over the years, she could have at least disliked Rebecca, but Shelly had never felt that way. Rebecca couldn't help it if she was one of those women put on earth to make other women feel inadequate. She was elegantly beautiful, incredibly poised and had impeccable political connections, as well as a wealthy family. All that, and she still managed to be a nice woman.

Shelly had no doubt that she would have been Rebecca's best friend if she hadn't known, almost from the beginning, that Brian was in love with Rebecca.

And now she was marrying someone else? It was simply unthinkable.

Shelly finally managed to slide the invitation out of the envelope and read the blasted thing.

> Samuel and Margaret Harwell request the honor of your presence at the marriage of their daughter, Ms. Rebecca Harwell, to Mr. Tucker Malloy...

Tucker Malloy?

Dear God, Shelly thought, this must be killing Brian.

Losing Rebecca was bad enough, but to lose her twice to the same man...

Chapter 3

Friday dawned warm and clear with a slight breeze, a perfect day for flying—unless you were Shelly Wilkerson.

She was going away with a man she should be avoiding at all costs. She had voluntarily closeted herself with him for a couple of hours in a plane with a cockpit that was smaller than the inside of her car. She was going to what had to be the wedding from hell with Brian, to see his ex-fiancée marry her ex-husband.

"You didn't tell me who she was marrying," Shelly said, having to shout to be heard over the noise of the engine.

"Would you have believed me?" he asked, turning away from the controls of the tiny two-seater plane for a moment to face her.

"No," she said. "I'm still having a hard time believing it myself."

Tucker Malloy was the man Rebecca had married before, the slick, hotshot lawyer who'd joined Rebecca's father's law firm at the same time he'd moved in on the boss's daughter.

Shelly had never been sure whether or not she liked Tucker, though nine years ago there was no one in Tallahassee who could have been more thrilled at the idea of another man marrying Rebecca. Tucker had always seemed a little too sure of himself, a little too handsome and almost untouchable.

Shelly would have bet money that no one had ever touched Tucker Malloy's soul, and what woman wanted a man whose soul she couldn't touch?

But Rebecca had married him, though it hadn't lasted long. Less than two years later, when their son, Sammy, had only been a few months old, they'd separated. Tucker Malloy left town, and as far she knew he'd never come back, despite the fact that his son lived in Tallahassee.

Brian had been more of a father to Sammy than Tucker ever had.

What had happened? Shelly wondered silently. What in the world had happened between Brian, Rebecca and Tucker? Less than a year ago, Brian had been engaged to Rebecca, and now the woman was marrying her ex-husband again?

"I'm sorry, Brian," she said, barely managing to get the words out. "I'm so sorry—"

"Don't be," he said, cutting her off.

Shelly touched him for the first time in years, putting her hand on his arm, wishing she dared to let herself do more than that. "Can I just . . . feel badly for you because . . ."

God, she'd be a fool to say any more.

She loved him. And even if she couldn't stand the idea of him marrying another woman, she hated seeing him hurt like this all the same.

"If you need someone to talk to . . ." She offered.

"I'd come to you, Shelly. But there's not that much to tell. Out of the blue, Tucker called Rebecca one night last summer. He said he wanted to see Sammy.

"He started coming to visit on weekends, and—aw, hell! I don't know. I just don't know. They're getting back together. End of story."

But it wasn't. It couldn't be that simple. Brian wouldn't have given up without a fight. And from the way Rebecca and Tucker's first marriage had ended, she couldn't imagine the two of them getting back together, despite the fact that they had a small child together.

There was a lot more to that story than Brian was telling, but Shelly didn't want to pry. He'd tell her, in time. He always did.

"I just... I wish there was something I could do," she said, having to settle for that.

"You're doing it. You're coming to the wedding with me."

Yes, the wedding . . .

"Wait a minute," she said to Brian as this awful thought came to her. "How did you get invited to this wedding?"

Brian didn't say a word.

Shelly couldn't believe she hadn't thought of it sooner, but the week had been absolutely crazy. "You're asking me to crash your ex-fiancée's wedding with you?"

It was laughable, really, but neither of them had cracked a smile.

"Actually," he said. "I was hoping you'd been invited and you'd take me."

"What a rotten thing to do," she said. "Rebecca will be furious. She'll never forgive me for this."

"Sure she will."

"Brian, that's outrageous!"

"Look, if Rebecca's going to stand at the altar and marry that man again, she's going to have to walk past me to do it."

His voice had been quite calm as he said it, and absolutely determined. He wouldn't be talked out of this, and she wondered what else he had planned.

"Brian—"

"I'm sorry, Shel." He didn't yell this time. He leaned toward her and his breath teased her ear, leaving her more unsettled than the conversation. "I shouldn't have gotten you in the middle of this mess. But I'm glad to have you with me." He took her hand in his, then pulled it away slightly so he could run his thumb over her sweaty palm.

She was nervous. He'd teased her about being afraid to fly, but that wasn't the problem, though she was just as happy to have him think it was. He made her nervous. Being in his company for the entire weekend was going to be harder than she thought.

"Are we almost there?"

"Another fifteen minutes or so. Think you can hang on that long?"

Maybe.

Or maybe she'd jump for it instead. It would probably be safer than being with him.

"I'll manage," she said, giving up on the idea of relaxing as his palm once again settled on hers and their fingers became intertwined.

"I am glad you came with me," he said as he squeezed her hand.

"Brian, I don't know if this—"

Shelly stopped when she realized she was shouting and didn't need to. The engine noise that had made conversation so difficult had finally quietened and the plane shifted, heading downward.

"Are we there already?"

"No."

She'd been looking to the side at a fluffy white cloud in an otherwise startlingly blue sky, but something in Brian's tone had her turning to face him.

The hand that had been holding hers was busy elsewhere now. He was calmly flipping switches and turning dials, quietly cursing as he worked his way across the control panel of the little plane.

Obviously they were in some kind of trouble.

"What's wrong?" she finally managed to ask.

"The engine's acting funny," he said tersely, concentrating on the instrument panel in front of him.

She held on a little tighter, then had a terrible thought. She'd never been in a plane this small, and she couldn't remember— "How many engines do we have?"

"One."

"One?" Shelly braced herself as best she could, but it wasn't enough. She put a hand to her suddenly queasy stomach and looked out the side window, wondering if little planes came with those bags you found in the seat in front of you on a big plane, just in case.

Of course, big planes had three or four engines, too, she reasoned.

Her search proving to be futile, she gave up on the barf bag and turned back to the window, looking to see how far they had to fall. It wasn't as far as she thought. They'd been flying low along the coastline the whole way until a few minutes ago when they'd turned inland to head for Tallahassee.

"The ground's getting closer," she announced, just in case he didn't realize.

"I know." His voice was as steady as it had been a second ago.

"Don't we want it the other way?" she said, fighting to keep the fear out of her voice, as well. "Don't we want to stay up?"

"Not if the engine's going to quit."

And then it did.

Near silence filled the plane, the loudest silence she'd ever heard.

Brian tried to get the engine to turn over again, but it sputtered a few times and died. "See anything down there that I could use for a runway?" he asked, working quickly but calmly over the controls.

Shelly saw trees, lots of trees—thick, tall, spindly pines.

"You've got to be kidding," she said.

"I never kid when my plane's going down."

She should have realized that if the engine quit, the plane would go down, but she was too busy fighting the urge to throw up. She really was afraid of flying, although right now that seemed foolish. The thing she feared was crashing.

And they would crash. Shelly looked down again. They had a long way to fall, but they were too low to give them much time at all. And there were all those trees in their way.

"We're going to crash," she said, certain of it now as she waited for the panic to set in.

"We're going to land a little hard," Brian said, sounding so matter-of-fact about it that she actually wondered for a minute if she was being foolish to be so scared.

And then she realized it had been a joke. How could he make a joke at a time like this? How could he be so damned calm?

She knew they were in for something worse than a rough landing, maybe something much worse. She thought about how foolish she'd been when it came to him and how much precious time they'd both wasted.

Maybe she should tell him how she felt, she thought, her mind racing from one thing to another. She'd always wondered what it would feel like to tell him. Shelly waited for her life to flash before her eyes. Wasn't that what was supposed to happen? But it just didn't come.

Instead, she heard Brian say, "Hell, there's nothing but trees down there."

And then she really got scared.

Brian got on the radio and broadcast a distress call along with their location, then turned his attention back to the ground.

There was nothing but trees. They couldn't land in the trees.

"Can we get back to the gulf?"

"No."

She tried again. "How far are we from the airport?"

"Too far."

Maybe she should tell him that she loved him. What harm would it do? On the other hand, what good would it do, either? It wasn't as if they'd have anything of a future together.

Shelly talked herself out of it again and turned back to the treetops. They were getting closer now. She could make out the leaves on the trees. Pines, with a few oaks interspersed among them.

The plane was moving slower and slower, and Brian was struggling to keep the nose up, to buy them a few more moments.

So she had time to wonder, again, if he'd laugh in her face if she told him how she felt about him. Shelly closed her eyes and tried to imagine his expression when she said it. He'd be shocked probably, though he'd try not to show it because he wouldn't want to hurt her feelings. And then she feared he wouldn't know what to say. What could he say, when he didn't feel the same way?

The plane lurched sickeningly beneath them, turning her stomach alarmingly.

Brian swore, and Shelly was scared to open her eyes. They had to be so close to the trees now. But she managed to open them, because she wanted to get one more look at his face. He had dark hair, dark eyes, a hint of Spanish blood that was evident in the darkness of his skin.

Shelly looked at the long, muscular length of his arms, now fighting desperately for control of the plane, and thought about the way she'd always longed for them to hold her. She looked at his lips, compressed into a thin line now, and she thought about the way she'd longed for him to kiss her. She thought of all the opportunities she'd let pass her by, of all the time she'd wasted, and vowed that if they got out of this alive, she'd make the most of every moment with him.

She must have made some sound because Brian turned to face her for a second. He must have seen the glimmer of tears in her eyes because he took his hands off the controls for a precious second or two so he could squeeze her hand.

"Hang on, Shel. It's not over yet."

It steadied her the way nothing could have. She'd always known she'd trust him with her life, and she did. He hadn't given up, and she wouldn't, either.

"Okay," she said, turning away for a moment to try to pull herself together.

That's when she saw the road.

"Brian," she said cautiously. She was afraid to believe her eyes. "Over there, to the right. There's—is it a road?"

"Where?"

"There!"

He was practically in her lap as he leaned across her to get a better look.

"Told you it wasn't over yet." He eased back into his seat and continued his fight with the controls. The man simply never gave up. "See any cars?"

She hadn't even thought about cars; she'd been so giddy with relief. "No, no cars."

"We're in business, then. Hang on." He pulled the plane into a wide, easy turn. "We're going to hit hard, and when we do, don't tense up. You'll hurt yourself even more that way. Just try to go with it."

She swallowed hard, wanting to ask just how hard it was to land a plane with no power. But if anyone could do it, he could. Brian was a rock. He always had been. When she was six, she'd been sure that nothing really bad could happen to her when he was close by. She wasn't naive enough to believe that now. But she knew there was no one she would trust more with her life than this man.

"Can we make it to the road?" she said.

"I think so."

He struggled with the wheel of the plane, and her breath caught in her throat as the treetops filled her vision.

She gasped, but his curses drowned out the sound.

The plane bounced a little as it scraped the tips of the trees, then miraculously settled in a line over the road, which came rushing up to meet them.

Brian pulled the plane hard to the left to make up for the brush with the treetops on the right. He overcompensated, and the plane hit the road at an angle, up on its left side, then banged again as the right wheels came down.

They bounced down the road, her head knocking against the side window, her vision clouding for a moment. But she didn't care. They were on the ground.

He'd gotten them to the ground.

Shelly was simply glad to be alive and ridiculously happy that she hadn't blurted out her feelings for him in a moment of panic.

Then she saw the water.

"Oh, my God," she gasped.

"Just our luck," Brian said, still struggling to control an uncontrollable situation. "We found the road that goes to the river."

It dead-ended in a parking lot and a boat ramp, one with no cars now, no boats, no people, no help.

He hit the brakes hard, but the plane didn't stop. It skidded drunkenly toward the end of the road.

The murky water filled her vision. She screamed when they hit harder than she expected. She'd thought they'd slowed down a lot more than they actually had, and she'd thought before that they'd be so much better off in the water than the trees.

And then she must have blacked out—either that or everything started to happen too fast, because the next thing she knew she was in the water. The water was inside the plane, filling it up, and she couldn't get loose.

"Brian!" She hoped she hadn't screamed his name.

"I'm here," he said, and she tried to beat back the panic that threatened to overtake her.

"I can't get out."

She was struggling with the unfamiliar buckle of the seat belt, and for a minute they struggled together when his hands closed over hers. She didn't understand at first, in her panic, that he was trying to help her.

Of course, he would help her.

She told herself that over and over again as he took over the struggle with the belt. The water rose faster than she would have believed. It was so cold on her legs, then her stomach.

"Brian," she said, the panic back, stronger than ever.

Then the belt came free, even as the water swirled around her chest. She had to untangle herself from the belt and push up to the ceiling—that was the only spot where the water hadn't reached.

"Shelly?" Brian's face came up out of the water right beside hers. "Listen to me. We've got to get out of here. I have to get the door open, and when I do, the water's going to come rushing in and we have to get out. Understand?"

Oh, yes, she understood. Shelly gasped for air, thinking about how much she hated to be underwater, even when she dove into a pool.

"Wait a minute," she said when he would have disappeared into the murky black of the swirling water.

He did, waiting there while the water closed in around them. There was so much she wanted to say, but at the moment, she couldn't get any of the words out of her mouth. So she just held out her arms to him and pulled him to her, holding him desperately for as long as he would allow it.

"It's going to be okay," he said, making her believe him. "We're going to get out of here."

Gently, but determinedly, he pulled free of her hold and told her what they had to do.

"When I get the door open, head for the door. You'll have to feel your way because it's going to be dark. Okay? Can you do it?"

She barely had a chance to nod.

"Okay, let's do it. I'm going to count to three. Take a couple more deep breaths, and when I get the door open, follow me. If you get lost, breathe out and follow your bubbles to the surface, all right?"

She would have protested, but he didn't give her time.

"One," he started counting, bobbing in the water as he did. She did the same, watching his eyes and trying to fight back the panic while she waited for the moment.

She truly hated being underwater. Swimming was all right, but going down below the surface for anything, even just a dive, was torture to her. The water always seemed so heavy, like it was going to crush her any minute.

"Two," he said, and her lungs already felt as if they were going to burst.

She was going to tell him. She had to.

"Three."

"Ahh," she screamed in protest, instead of breathing as she'd been told.

And then he was gone.

"I love you, Brian," she said, too late for him to hear. "And if we get out of this mess alive, I'm going to tell you."

She heard the door give way, saw the water rush in and then there was no time for anything else. She made a wild grab for air and followed him down into the murky river water.

Shelly woke up in Brian's arms on the bank of the river, unsure how she got there, unsure for a moment what had happened.

And then she saw the plane, just the tail, sticking out of the water.

Her stomach rolled. She shivered in the cool wind coming off the river, then tried to snuggle closer to him. She hadn't been this close to him in years. She just couldn't stop shaking, and her head felt as if it had been split in two.

"Ouch," she said when she tried to sit up and everything started spinning in little circles around the center of the pain in her head.

"Relax," Brian said, and his voice helped her to do just that. "You don't need to go anywhere."

She coughed up a little water, and that hurt even more—her head was spinning and her lungs burned.

"What happened?"

"You must have banged your head getting out of the plane, and you blacked out for a minute. Swallowed a little water, too."

And damned near gave him a heart attack in the process.

Brian had surfaced and found nothing but the murky water and a sinking plane. No Shelly. And he'd been more frightened then than he had been when he realized that the engine had stopped and it wasn't going to start again.

He dove back under the water, found her limp and lifeless in the plane. And somehow he'd gotten her out, gotten her to cough up some water, and then he held her for what seemed like forever until she opened those pretty brown eyes of hers. His heart had settled down a little, but he still held her tight.

"God, Shelly!"

He held her tight enough that he could feel each breath she took as they both sat there, wet and cold, and watched the plane sink below the surface.

He could hear the sirens in the distance now, and he wondered how long it would be before they found them, wondered if he'd have to leave her here while he walked back down the road in search of some help. He didn't think he could leave her here, didn't think he could make himself let her go.

She'd been a part of his life forever, and somehow he'd known she always would be. She was one of the best friends he'd ever had, and he couldn't imagine losing her.

Brian looked at the bump on her head again and tried not to close his eyes, because when he did he kept seeing her floating lifelessly under the water, kept scaring himself all over again. So he just held on to her until the fire trucks and the ambulance came, and he had to finally let her go.

Chapter 4

Shelley woke up a little stiff and sore, a little dizzy, but otherwise whole, in a hotel bed the next morning.

It took her a while to remember why.

There was a dreamlike quality to the day before. Nightmarish, actually. She remembered the little plane, the noise of the engine and then the silence, all those trees and that black water, the panic, the pain and finally the sirens and a strong pair of arms wrapped around her, holding her close.

They'd almost died. She still had trouble believing it.

If Brian hadn't been able to find her in the plane—if he hadn't been able to pull her out of the water... She shuddered, just remembering the way the water had closed in around her, blinding her, pinning her down under its surface, robbing her lungs of air and leaving her head spinning as she fought helplessly to get away.

She couldn't have gotten away on her own. She'd gotten tangled up in the seats and the seat belts and she didn't even know what else. She'd just kept bumping into things as she'd tried to find the door. And the harder she'd tried to get out, the more frantic she'd become, the more useless her efforts had become.

Brian had saved her.

She closed her eyes and tried to calm herself. Her head still felt as if it had been split in two, and if she turned her head too quickly the room spun alarmingly. She lay back against the pillows and decided she could wait a minute or two before she made her way to the bathroom.

God, they had actually come close to dying.

She'd been certain she would die in those awful moments alone in the dark plane, with the water rising.

And then she'd come to and found herself on the riverbank, in Brian's arms. It had been so bittersweet—the way he'd held her. Had she imagined it, or had he been reluctant to let her go? Of course there was a reason, she realized, wincing at the memory of their conversation in this very bed, sometime deep in the night....

She was under the water, trapped there in the blackness, and she didn't know how to get out. It was cold and dark and heavy. She was running out of time, and the water was pressing against her, holding her down, almost paralyzing her.

"Brian!" she screamed, nearly jumping off the hotel bed. She would have jumped if he hadn't caught her in his arms.

"Hey," he crooned to her as he caught her hard against him. "It's all right. It's over. You're safe now."

"Ahh," she gasped, clinging to him with every bit of her strength. Her breath was coming in big gulps, and the pain was reverberating through her head with every beat of her heart.

"It's all right," Brain said again, settling himself on the bed so he could lean against the headboard. He pulled her back against him.

"I was in the water again," she said. It seemed that remembering was just as scary as living through the real thing. "I didn't think I was going to get out."

"Hey," Brian said, tightening his arms around her and pulling her closer than she'd been in years. "You're out. You're safe now."

She was. It was hard to believe, but she was safe and in a hotel suite in Tallahassee with him right beside her. But even now, knowing where she was, it was still hard to push away the terror of being trapped in that plane and unable to find the way out.

"It's all right, Shel," he said, the tenor of his voice dipping deeper and rougher than she'd ever heard it.

She started to tremble again, as badly as she had once he'd pulled her out of the water. She wasn't sure how she ever stopped the first time or how she would again. And it was so wonderful to have him hold her. She didn't want him to ever let go.

"I couldn't have gotten out by myself, Brian." She knew it was true. She had this irrational fear of being underwater, and she'd panicked when the time came to get herself out of that plane.

"Hush," he said. "It's over now."

She shook her head back and forth, then winced at the pain that movement brought on.

"You saved my life," she said, fighting against the urge to snuggle closer to him now that she was awake enough to know better. But the choice wasn't hers to make at that moment. His arms tightened around her, crushing her to him. She couldn't have moved if her life depended upon it.

"I didn't think I'd ever find you down there."

Shelly closed her eyes and wondered if someone, some-where, was finally going to answer her prayers. She lay there in his arms, afraid to move, afraid to breathe, afraid to hear what was coming next.

"I would have never forgiven myself if anything had happened to you," he said huskily.

Shelly held her breath as she waited for him to continue. She'd come so close to telling him yesterday, so close to just blurting out everything she felt for him.

She felt his lips kiss her softly on the forehead, felt his arms tighten around her for a moment before he pulled away, just far enough so that once he tilted her chin up toward his face, he could see her eyes.

"I couldn't stand the idea of losing you, Shel. You're like family to me—the closest thing to a sister I ever had."

Shelly felt the bottom drop out of her world—it was much like the feeling of the plane falling out of the sky. She smiled through her tears; she still had some pride left.

Loving this man was going to kill her someday.

She closed her eyes tight and tried to remember this feeling—hopes dashed yet again. She should remember it well because it never stopped where the two of them were concerned.

Slowly, carefully, she pulled away. She just couldn't stand to be this close to him for another moment.

"I think I need to lie down again," she said.

"Are you sure you're all right?" he asked before he let her go.

She nodded, then turned onto her side with her back to him. It was all she could manage.

Shelly rolled over in the bed and looked around, wanting to know for sure that she was alone in the bedroom of the suite. The big, overstuffed chair pulled to the side of the bed was empty now, and the door to the sitting room was closed.

She was grateful for just a few precious moments alone. She'd been so hopeful before that moment in the middle of the night—when he'd crushed her dreams of the two of them together.

He'd ridden in the ambulance beside her, holding her hand on the ride to the hospital in Tallahassee. He'd been at the hospital with her, and when the doctor had wanted to keep her overnight for observation, Brian had promised to watch over her during the night. It had been the only way the doctor would agree to let her leave the hospital.

Shelly hated hospitals. She'd spent a lot of time in them when she was little, when her mother had died. Brian probably knew that. Surely she would have told him about that sometime. All she knew was that she hadn't had to explain it to him last night. He'd simply understood and found a way to get her out of the hospital.

Neither one of them wanted to face his family last night and tell them what had happened. Exhausted and wanting nothing more than to rest, they'd checked into a suite at the Clairmont and decided to let the explanations wait until morning.

Now it was morning.

Even worse—it was Rebecca's wedding day. She was due to walk down the aisle in—Shelly squinted at the digital clock on the nightstand—eight and a half hours.

That and an urgent need to find the bathroom was enough to convince Shelly she had to get out of bed. Cautiously, slowly, she sat up on the side of the bed, then got to her feet and struggled to make it to the other side of the room.

After using the bathroom, she made her way to the mirror and groaned at the sight before her. She may have only come close to dying, but she looked as if she'd actually done it. There was an ugly bruise running along the side of her face, right up against the hairline, from cheekbone to temple. It was an angry reddish color now, but she'd probably be black-and-blue tomorrow.

Her arms were bruised, too, probably from when Brian had pulled her from the plane. Her brown, shoulder-length hair, which she normally kept under control in a loose braid hanging down her back, was going every which way, and she smelled of river water.

The lime-green scrub suit they'd given her to wear at the hospital did ghastly things for her skin. Normally pale, her complexion now took on a ghostly tint.

And her eyes were huge and red—lack of sleep and too many tears. She'd sobbed uncontrollably sometime in the night, with her head buried in a pillow to muffle the sound so Brian wouldn't hear.

Like family, he'd said. Like the sister he'd never had. She'd spent years daydreaming about a man who loved her like a sister, and if she wasn't careful she'd waste even more time doing that.

Shelly stripped off the drab green scrub suit, took a quick shower to wash off the scent of the river, then filled the big whirlpool tub with warm water and stepped into it. She listened to the gurgling sound of the bubbles rushing to the surface of the water, and she didn't cry this time. She was done with that. Once and for all, she was going to rip that man out of her heart.

Brian was waiting for her when she opened the bathroom door, and he didn't look at all like someone whose plane had crashed into a muddy river the day before.

Shelly knew she still looked that way, though.

"I didn't think you were ever going to wake up," he said.

She just stood there in nothing but the hotel's big, fluffy bathrobe and somehow endured having him sweep her hair aside so he could look at the bruising on her face.

"Still know what day it is?" he quizzed her, as he had throughout the night.

"Saturday."

"What state we're in?"

"Florida."

"Who the president of the United States is?"

"I voted for him—you didn't."

"I guess you're going to live," he said, trying to make a joke of it. He was worried about her. "How's your head?"

"Is it still in one piece?" She wasn't sure, judging from the way it felt

He nodded.

"Then I guess I can't complain."

She made her way over to the bed, groaning as she sat down on the edge of it.

"Sore?"

"Very."

"Me, too." He helped her swing around so her head was propped against the pillows and her feet were stretched out in front of her.

Shelly watched his hands as they settled back against his sides. She wondered what she'd have to do to keep them there—by his sides and off of her. She wondered how she could reconstruct some of that hard-won distance between them that she'd tried so hard to maintain, distance that had all but shattered in the past twelve hours or so.

She'd clung to him on the riverbank, in the ambulance, at the hospital and long into the night while he'd sat by her bedside and slept in the chair he occupied now. She needed the distance. She needed that desperately.

"Look," Brian said. "The doctor gave us some pills last night for the soreness. He said you could have some if you needed them once you woke up this morning. They're in the bathroom."

"I think I'll wait and see how I feel." Besides, she wanted to be as clearheaded as possible. "Does anyone know about the accident yet?"

"I called my parents. My mother dug some of my old clothes out of a closet at the house, and then she went out to pick up a few things for you. She should be back any minute now."

"Good, I was dreading putting that scrub suit back on." And she sure didn't want to sit around the hotel suite with him in nothing but this robe. God, this was so awkward. She asked herself, once again, how she'd gotten herself into this mess and how she was going to get out of it.

She was thinking of how to get out of this situation when he caught her off guard again. She'd looked away for a second, so she didn't see the hand that came out to gently tilt her chin to the left so he could look more closely at the bruise on her face.

It had always amazed her how gentle he could be. It wasn't a quality most men felt comfortable letting someone see, but he did.

"Are you sure you feel all right?" he asked, coming so close she felt his breath stirring the strands of hair that had escaped from her braid. He was watching her too intently as far as she was concerned.

What did he see? she wondered. Was he remembering the way she'd held on to him so desperately on the riverbank, the way she hadn't wanted to let go of his hand in the ambulance or at the hospital? Was he wondering why? Or did he already know how she felt about him? Maybe last night was his way of telling her that he didn't feel anything but a sisterly sort of affection for her.

Her face burned at the thought.

"I've had better days," she admitted at last, then searched her brain for something else they could discuss. "The plane? Did you figure out what went wrong?"

Brian shrugged, still not taking his eyes off her. "Not much. Not yet, anyway. I talked to Charlie this morning, too, and he said he'd just had the plane serviced because he was planning to take it to Saint Pete on Monday."

"So what could have happened?"

"I don't know. Charlie's a careful man. He takes good care of that machine. We'll probably have to have it hauled out of the river and let the mechanics run over it before we know for sure."

Brian's mother, Katherine Sandelle, was the epitome of a well-bred Southern lady who prided herself on her image and her gracious manners. But she was so shocked by Shelly's appearance, she could do nothing but stare at her. Her reaction was so obvious that Shelly wanted to run to the nearest mirror again and see if she could possibly look any worse than she had when she'd crawled out of bed this morning.

Surely that wasn't possible, Shelly reasoned, then hit on the real problem.

"Brian didn't tell you everything, did he?"

"Obviously not," she said, dropping her shopping bags on the floor and sitting down in the chair Brian had slept in. "Are you all right, dear?"

"I'm sure it looks worse than it is," Shelly said. "Really. I just have a big bruise, a splitting headache and lots of sore muscles."

"I think my son has some explaining to do," she said.

"What did he tell you?" Shelly asked, although she had a pretty good idea of what he would say.

"I believe his exact words were that the landing was a little rough and that you got bounced around a bit."

"He didn't say anything about losing the engine, landing on a little country road or running the plane into a river?" She still had trouble believing it.

Katherine Sandelle looked truly shocked then. "No."

"He probably wanted to wait until you were standing face-to-face before he sprung all that on you."

"He had that chance this morning when I brought him his clothes."

Shelly leaned back into the pillows that were holding up her aching head, and she shivered in the suddenly cool room as the scenes from the day before ran through her mind. She didn't want to remember. She didn't want to talk about it, but Brian's mother had a right to know some things.

"He was incredible up there in the plane. I don't think he knows the meaning of the word panic. And then when we landed in the river..." Shelly didn't care for the trembling quality of her own voice and paused to try to control it.

It was over. They'd survived, thanks to Brian.

"He saved my life," she told his mother. "He wouldn't ever tell you himself, but I want you to know that he saved me. The plane was sinking—it was nearly full of water. I got lost in the darkness, and I was scared. I couldn't find my way out of there."

Brian's mother was scared, too, now.

"He pulled me out of the plane, and he got me out of the water," Shelly said. "He was incredible."

"Well, I'm a little prejudiced, but I'd have to agree with you, dear." She took Shelly's hand in hers and gave it a squeeze. "Now tell me about you. We've missed you. You've stayed away much too long."

"I've missed you all, too," Shelly said, and it was true. She missed both Brian's parents and the big house that was so familiar to her. "I hope you don't think that I—"

A knock sounded on the outer door to the suite, and Shelly paused, unsure of what to do.

"I have a feeling I know who that is. We should let Brian get it," his mother said.

"Oh?"

"Rebecca and Sammy," she explained. "When Brian called this morning, he caught up with me at Rebecca's parents' house. They were there having the wedding breakfast. Sammy was a little concerned about Brian, and Rebecca promised to bring him over here for a minute."

"Oh," Shelly said, staring at the door that separated them from what was sure to be an awkward scene in the next room. "I don't...I don't know what to say. I feel so bad for Brian, and I don't understand how this could have happened...."

"He's going to be fine," his mother said.

"But Rebecca..."

"Rebecca doesn't love him the way a woman should love the man she marries."

Shelly was simply stunned. She'd always know that Brian and Rebecca belonged together. She thought everyone did, especially his own mother.

"Shelly, dear, I know Brian's been hurt by all this, and I'm sorry for that. But it's been more than five years since Rebecca's divorce from Tucker was final. If she'd truly wanted to marry Brian, she would have done it long before now. If Brian didn't have such a blind spot where she was concerned, he would have figured it out for himself long ago."

Shelly couldn't say anything. Katherine Sandelle and Margaret Harwell, Rebecca's mother, were the best of friends; they had been for years. Shelly had assumed that the two of them had been plotting and planning to marry off their children forever. She had been sure Brian's mother would have been as upset as Brian was by the thought of Rebecca marrying someone else. But clearly she wasn't.

"Brian's going to be fine once he accepts what's happened," Katherine said.

"I'm sure he will," Shelly said. "I just... I hate to see him hurt this way."

"Really, he's going to be fine. And now that Rebecca's getting married, he'll find someone, too. And he'd better hurry. His father and I are ready to start spoiling our grandchildren."

Shelly hadn't even thought of that. Of course he would find someone, or more likely, some other woman would find him.

When Brian had first moved to Naples, they'd had a temp working in one of the secretarial positions at the engineering firm. The woman had been disappointed to learn that he was engaged, but it hadn't stopped her from going after him.

Shelly had hated the woman for it. And there'd be nothing to stop women like that from going after him now. She couldn't watch that, she decided. She couldn't be there and see him with another woman.

"You know, my dear," Brian's mother said. "When you were six years old, you were sure that one day you were going to marry my son."

Shelly stammered and stuttered around her words for a minute, and then just gave up and closed her mouth. What could she say? She had wanted to marry the man forever. But she didn't know his mother knew that, too.

"We were children," she finally managed to say.

"But you're not anymore."

She said it so matter-of-factly, as if it wouldn't bother her if her son did marry Shelly.

Amazing, Shelly thought. She truly liked Katherine Sandelle, and the woman was no snob. Still, even the most openminded person had to have second thoughts about her son marrying the daughter of her former grounds keeper.

Shelly saw no signs of that coming from the woman now.

Did that mean she wouldn't object—assuming there ever was anything between the two of them? Did she know how Shelly still felt? Did the whole world know how she felt about him, as well?

"Well, I really have to be going." Katherine Sandelle handed Shelly a mountain of shopping bags. "Brian said you didn't have anything to wear, so I picked up a few things for you."

"Thank you," Shelly said, still stunned by what she'd heard.

"Is there another way out of here? I don't think I want to get in the middle of that meeting in the next room."

Shelly wasn't sure herself. The night before was a blur, but she looked around and found a door. "Through there?"

"That's it," Brian's mother said. "See you at the wedding, dear."

Shelly watched her go, then made her way to the door that led to the living room of the suite and cautiously opened it. She wanted to know if Brian still intended to go to this wedding, but she didn't want to see him with Rebecca.

Just her luck, she caught him as he was saying goodbye.

She watched while Brian stooped down far enough that he was eye level with Rebecca's six-year-old son and gave the boy a big hug.

"I've missed you, Brian," she heard Sammy say.

"I miss you, too, buddy."

Sammy was a cutie, and he looked so much like his father, Tucker. She wondered how in the world Brian had handled that over the years he'd spent being a substitute father to Sammy. Every time he looked at the boy, he had to be reminded of the man Rebecca had married.

And yet from what she saw now, he and Sammy seemed to be incredibly close. The little boy had tears in his eyes as he clung to Brian.

Shelly didn't want to see or hear this, but something kept her glued to the spot. From the doorway, she watched as Sammy stepped into the hallway and Brian and Rebecca stood at arm's length from each other, their clasped hands between them. Rebecca looked stunning as always.

Shelly couldn't see Brian's face, and she was glad of that. But she could sense the tension in the room.

"I'm sorry, Brian," she heard Rebecca say.

"I hope you know what you're doing," he said.

"I do. I'm certain of it."

Brian didn't say anything more. He kissed her lightly on the cheek, squeezed her hands once, and then she was gone.

Shelly closed the door behind her and stood with her back to it, shaking like a leaf, knowing exactly what that had to have cost him.

She was still standing there beside the connecting door when, a moment later, someone knocked on the outer door. She thought that Brian's mother must have forgotten something. She certainly never expected to find Rebecca and her little boy standing there.

"Hi," Shelly said, wishing she'd never opened that door.

"Hello," Rebecca said, looking as beautiful and as elegant as always. "I was worried about you. Brian told me about the plane, and he said you were hurt. Are you all right?"

Shelly nodded, letting herself be drawn into a quick hug.

"I saw you standing by the other door," Rebecca said. "And I . . . I don't mean to pry, but I just wanted to tell you that I'm glad you're here with Brian. And I—"

"Oh, it's not— It's not anything like that," Shelly said, stumbling over the words in her haste to get them out.

"Oh." Rebecca just smiled. "Of course. I just worry about him, still. He's a very special man."

"I know."

"I always thought that you...well, that you felt that way about him, too."

Shelly tilted her chin up just a fraction of an inch. Did the whole world know how she felt about Brian? It was starting to seem that way.

"Look, I really didn't mean to pry," Rebecca said. "I just wanted to make sure you were all right."

Shelly nodded, unable to find anything to say to the woman, feeling as if someone might as well have plastered her feelings all over a billboard for the whole town to see.

"Well, I guess we'd better be going. It was good to see you again, Shelly."

"Yes," she managed to get out. "It was good to see you, too."

And with that, Rebecca turned to the quiet little boy standing beside her and said, "Come on, Sammy. We've got to get ready."

Shelly figured her day couldn't get any worse, unless Brian was still determined to go to the wedding.

Chapter 5

Brian shifted on the uncomfortable church pew. The muscles in his neck and his shoulders were clenching tighter with every passing moment.

"This is a mistake," Shelly said as the organist finally paused in preparation for the beginning of the ceremony.

"I know. I figured that out sometime last night," Brian said, tugging impatiently at the tie his father had loaned him. His own clothes were probably still at the bottom of the river. The county emergency team was having trouble hauling the plane out of the water.

"So why are we here?" Shelly said.

"Sammy nailed me on it this morning at the hotel. Said he wanted me to come, and I promised I would. He's excited. He thinks it's going to be *fun*."

Shelly had to laugh. He said the last word as if it were an obscenity.

"Well, you're the one who wanted to be here," she reminded him. "And you are. You even managed to get yourself invited."

"I swear we're drawing more attention than Rebecca will when she walks down the aisle. Everybody in the whole place is staring at us," he said.

"They probably want to see what happens when Tucker spots you. Either that, or they want to see if you're going to jump up and yell when the minister asks if anyone knows of any reason why Tucker and Rebecca shouldn't be married."

Brian did smile then.

"You wouldn't," she said.

"No, but I like the idea of Tucker wondering if I would."

If coming to the wedding was a mistake, coming to the reception was a colossal one.

At least at the church, people pretty much kept to themselves and stayed fairly quiet. At the reception on the patio of Rebecca's parents' home, there was altogether too much mixing and mingling and conversation.

Brian put a hand to the back of his neck and pulled at the ever-tightening muscles there. He hadn't felt that bad this morning, but the stiffness was setting in with a vengeance now. He'd taken a couple of aspirin before coming to the church, but they hadn't seemed to help. So he finally gave in and fished around in his pockets for the painkillers the doctor had given him the night before.

He swallowed two and tried not to frown as the bride and groom arrived and the guests lined up to greet them.

"We're not going through the receiving line," Shelly said, sticking close to him.

"That would be incredibly rude," he said, tucking her arm through his. He was enjoying her attempts to protect him. No one but Shelly had ever tried to do that.

"Getting slugged by the groom while you try to kiss the bride would be incredibly rude. Avoiding the reception line altogether would be a smart move."

"I kissed the bride this morning," he said, causing something of a stir when the couple behind him overheard what he'd said.

"Oh, great," Shelly said. She watched as the couple whispered among themselves, the news spreading through the crowd. "Wait till that gets back to the groom."

Brian suspected the groom already knew, and maybe he was still mad enough over this whole situation to find some pleasure in that, contemptible as that might be. But he had to admit that, overall, he hadn't gotten nearly the satisfaction he'd expected out of coming to this wedding. He'd tried to convince himself that Rebecca was marrying her ex-husband out of some misguided need to put the family back together again for her son's sake.

He didn't believe that now.

He wanted to watch her walk down the aisle and have her know that he was there, watching her, wanting her to reconsider every decision she'd made in the past six months even as she made her way to the altar. If she had any doubts about her decision, Brian wanted them to all come to the surface at that moment.

But they hadn't. She hadn't hesitated when it came time to recite her vows. For the life of him, he'd never understand it, but Rebecca seemed to have fallen in love with Tucker all over again.

Brian had watched her when she talked about the man, had watched her say her vows, and he had to admit that she'd never looked at him the way she was looking at Tucker now.

Hell, maybe it wasn't such a total loss, after all. It galled him to admit it, but he couldn't deny it, either. Maybe that's why he needed to come—to see for himself what she felt for her new husband. He couldn't deny it any longer, and he'd damn sure wasted enough of his life pursuing this woman. At least after watching the scene unfolding before him, he wouldn't waste another day of his life thinking about Rebecca Malloy.

Shelly came up to his side and slipped her hand into his, which he realized must have been clenched tight in a fist.

"Seen enough?" she asked.

"More than."

"Then we don't need to be here any longer, do we?"

No, he didn't.

"Hey," he said, squeezing her hand. "I'm sorry I dragged you into the middle of this whole mess. But I'm glad you came with me."

"Anytime," she said.

"Anytime I get dumped, huh?" That put a smile on her face, and for a minute she didn't look so pale. "You feel all right?"

"My head still hurts a little," she said.

He could see the beginnings of a nasty bruise that was forming on the side of her face, despite the way she'd tried to hide it beneath some makeup. Her head had to be aching, too, but she'd come with him, anyway. And she looked incredible in the soft pink suit his mother brought her.

It surprised him sometimes to see her like this—all grown up. Sometimes, he still thought of her as a little girl.

"Let's go," he said, holding tight to her hand. They dodged friends and family as best they could as they crossed the crowded room, spoke briefly to those who wouldn't be put off.

They were almost to the door when they got waylaid yet again, this time by a waiter armed with a tray full of champagne.

The music died down. The crowd turned toward the left side of the room where Rebecca's father held his glass high in the air, his booming voice reaching to the far corners of the room.

"Damn!" Brian said. Caught for the moment, they gave in to the age-old custom of toasting the bride and groom.

Brian still felt as if half the eyes in the room were on him. He downed one glass of champagne and, as the toasting went on, he snagged another from a passing waiter. Halfway through the round of toasts, he realized that his neck didn't hurt anymore. The pain in his shoulder had eased up on him, too.

Maybe the champagne toasts would be good for something, after all. He grabbed another glass and managed to smile at the happy couple.

Rebecca was a stunning bride, he decided, totally objectively. He'd always known she would be. With his best poker face on, he watched the groom give her a kiss, then took another sip of the champagne. Though he despised the taste, it was blurring the sight before him.

By the time the toasting was over, his head was spinning.

Brian had borrowed his mother's car this morning to drive them to the wedding. When the dancing started, he gave the keys to Shelly, and he didn't remember a lot after that.

Except dancing.

He remembered dancing—in this strange, surreal sort of world.

Except he wasn't at the reception. *They* weren't at the reception.

He wasn't sure where they were, and he didn't care, either. He had her in his arms, spinning her around the room and then pulling her back into his arms while this slow, sexy saxophone crooned in the background.

She loved jazz, and he loved having her this close.

The music changed; it slowed, and so did they. She swayed against him, barely, in time to the music.

She was here, where she belonged, with him.

He felt the blood pooling in his loins, felt it rushing there with every sway of her body against his. He caught her hips in his hands and settled her body intimately against his.

It felt so good, so right.

He nuzzled her cheek, teasing her, taunting her, until finally she gave him her mouth.

It had been so long since they'd been together.

He'd been afraid that they would never be together again, and here they were. He wasn't ever going to let her go this time.

Her jacket had these big pear buttons on it. He undid them one by one, then eased it off her shoulders and down, just a little, trapping her arms at her sides and freeing the sensuous curves of the tops of her breasts. He started tracing that curve with his mouth, and then couldn't help groaning aloud. Brian sank to his knees and buried his face in that heavenly soft hollow between her small, delicate breasts.

Her knees bucked, and he held her up where she was and teased her breasts until she begged him to let her go.

But he didn't let her go far.

They sank down to the floor and rolled across the carpet as they struggled with their clothes, laughing and kissing as they went.

He liked the music, loved the sweet smell of her skin—he breathed in deeply and pulled it down into his lungs.

He liked the way the song slowed to this incredibly erotic beat, the way he was thrusting into her in time to the music, hoping against hope that he could make it last, even as he knew it wouldn't.

It couldn't.

It was just too good; he knew it as he slid into her one more time, the last time, and called her name.

Rebecca!

Brian wasn't sure why and he wasn't at all sure about this, but he thought she slapped him then.

It was all pretty much a blur the next morning as it unfolded ever so slowly.

First, he remembered the champagne. How the hell many glasses had he had?

He felt awful, and he was having trouble putting a coherent thought together. It felt as if his brain hadn't been used in years, and the dust and the cobwebs had taken it over. He couldn't seem to make his way through all the muck.

He remembered the wedding.

Damn, was it only yesterday? How long had he been out?

Brian rolled over in the bed, not even sure where he was until he saw the little sign advertising the room-service specialties with the hotel logo on top of it.

He was at the Clairmont.

He remembered deciding to keep the suite for the weekend. His parents lived next door to Rebecca's, where the wedding reception was, and he didn't care to be that close to the festivities.

Yes, he remembered the wedding, the reception, the champagne, the dream.

He saw it all, as well as he could, despite the haze in his brain and the way the room didn't turn quite as fast as his head did.

Damn, what a dream. He got hard just thinking about it. Hell of a way to spend a wedding night—dreaming about rolling around on the floor with another man's bride.

Brian tried to get up, but laid back down as fast as he could. His head hurt. His neck still hurt, and he couldn't quite separate reality from fantasy, the dream from the—

He remembered the pills then.

Damn, what a stupid thing to do, mixing the two. He hadn't worried about taking the pills, because he hadn't intended to have anything to drink. But once they'd gotten caught by the toasts, he completely forget about those pills. He knew he couldn't have stood in the middle of all those curious people and not toasted the bride right along with the rest of them.

Brian tried, again, to get up and go to the bathroom. His head was going to split in two, and his stomach rolled alarmingly. The stiffness in his muscles had returned, worse than the day before, but there was no way he was popping another one of those little pills.

He made it to the bathroom and stared at himself through bloodshot eyes. He couldn't tell if he looked as bad as he felt, because the image in the mirror was swaying alarmingly. He could tell that he was naked, which he found a little unsettling.

He did seem to be in one piece, which was more than he could expect after what he'd done. Other than a stiff neck and shoulder and a pounding head, he was okay.

Somehow he managed to make it into the shower and turned it on full blast, cold as hell, desperately trying to clear his head. He fumbled with the soap, dropping it on the shower floor. Bending over to pick it up was hell on his head and his shoulder, but he finally managed it.

Funny, he thought, smoothing the little bar of soap across his chest, he could almost smell the woman's scent on his skin.

After showering and soaking in the whirlpool tub until some of the stiffness in his muscles went away, he walked out of the bedroom and into the living room of the suite. Shelly was there. He thought she must have been asleep because she practically jumped out of the big wingback chair in the corner when he walked into the room.

"Hi," he said, rubbing at his aching head.

"Hi." She didn't look at him when she said it. She just stood there in the middle of the room.

She'd showered and dressed. One of the shopping bags his mother had brought yesterday sat at her feet, stuffed full of things. She was much too pale, her skin taking on this clear-as-glass appearance. It left her looking fragile as hell. The bruise on the side of her face didn't help, either. It had darkened overnight, and it was bigger than he expected it to be.

She finally turned to face him, and he thought she must have been crying in the not-too-distant past.

What in the world was wrong with her?

"Shel?" he said, and she quickly turned away. How strange.

She didn't say anything. She didn't do anything, just hugged her arms to her chest and kept her face averted from his.

"Thanks for bringing me back to the hotel last night," he said cautiously.

She shot him a look of pure venom. Her eyes went all cold, but her cheeks flushed bright red. He detected a definite chill in the atmosphere, and he had a bad feeling about this.

"You did bring me back here, didn't you?"

"Yes," she said, as if she couldn't believe he was asking.

He must have been totally out of it last night. "It was the pills...." he said, knowing that didn't excuse whatever he'd done, but hoping it might at least help explain.

"What?" she cried.

"The pills—the ones the doctor gave us—the muscle relaxers. My neck and my shoulders were killing me once we got to the church, and I finally took a couple. I guess they don't mix well with champagne."

"Pills?" Shelly felt his eyes on her, felt her cheeks burning and wondered if he'd noticed. She couldn't believe this had happened to her, but at the same time she couldn't believe she'd gotten so lucky on this point. He didn't remember.

Maybe there was a god, and Brian didn't remember.

She'd thought he was just drunk—which had puzzled her, because it was unlike him. She'd been beside him the whole time at the reception, and she didn't think he'd drunk any more champagne than she had. She hadn't even gotten tipsy from it.

"Shelly?" He seemed fine now, and he was staring at her as if he were trying to look right inside her, as if he knew she was hiding something from him and he intended to find out what it was. "What's wrong?"

"Nothing," she said, backing away a step for every one he took toward her.

"What happened here last night?"

"You passed out," she lied with a totally clear conscience. "I left you in the bed to sleep it off."

"Did you take my clothes off, too?"

She knew she turned beet red at that and stammered something about the bellman, the one who helped her drag him up to the suite.

"Come on, Shel." He looked really worried now.

She had to get out of this room.

"Brian, I have to go. I've... I have a cab waiting, and... I have some things to take care of. I'll see you back in Naples."

"Wait a minute," he said, catching her by the arm when she tried to slip past him.

Shelly looked down at the hand on her arm, at the man still dripping from the shower, naked except for the towel wrapped precariously around his waist. She had to get out of here.

"I have to go," she said, knowing she couldn't unless he decided to let her go, praying that he would.

The phone rang, drawing both their eyes. But neither of them moved to answer it. He held her arm. She refused to meet his eyes. In the space of a dozen frantic beats of her heart, the phone rang again, then a third time.

Brian cursed and let go of her long enough to cross the room to the phone and lift the receiver to his ear.

She was halfway to the door by the time he turned around.

"Shelly," he said, only half listening to the voice coming through the phone. "Wait a minute. Shel?"

He would have dropped the phone and chased her down the hallway, towel and all, until he heard the man on the other end of the phone say something about the plane crash.

"What?" he said, sure that he'd heard the man wrong.

And then, for a few moments at least, he forgot all about going after Shelly.

Chapter 6

He wasn't on the phone for two minutes. Inside of five, he was dressed and out the door, hoping he wasn't too late to catch her.

She wasn't in the lobby, and she wasn't at the entranceway, although there was a transportation company van pulling out of the circular driveway when he got outside.

"Hey," he said, catching the bell captain. "Is that van going to the airport?"

He wasn't sure she'd have the nerve to fly again so soon after the accident, but it would be the fastest way to get out of town. And the lady seemed very interested in getting out of town.

"You just missed it," the man said. "But the next one will be along in twenty minutes or so."

"Was a woman on there? In her twenties, light brown hair, comes down to her shoulders?"

The man knew right away. "Great legs and no luggage. Just a shopping bag?"

Brian couldn't say he'd ever really noticed her legs, but the shopping bag clinched it. "That's her."

"She was on the van."

"She didn't happen to mention what airline she was taking, did she?"

The bellman laughed and looked him over a little more carefully. "Guess you're in the doghouse, man."

Brian tried to smooth down his wet hair, then decided it was time to finish buttoning his shirt, too.

Here he was, half-dressed, his hair sticking up, chasing a woman with no luggage out of a hotel on Sunday morning. He guessed that pretty much told the story.

He hoped it didn't.

"Yeah, I'm in trouble," he said, praying for all he was worth that he'd done nothing more than kiss her and call her Rebecca.

Surely things hadn't gone as far as they had in his dream. She'd never forgive him if they had. He'd never forgive himself.

"Help me out here," Brian said to the man. "I have to catch that woman."

The man sized him up once again. "She didn't say what airline she was flying, but she was worried about making the flight. She said it leaves at eight-thirty."

Brian checked his watch. Less than forty minutes. He prayed the plane would be late, that traffic would be light, that she'd give him a chance to explain. He prayed that nothing much had happened and he didn't have that much to explain to her.

"I need a cab," Brian told the man, pulling out a bill and pressing it into the man's hand. "I'll be back in three minutes, and I need to get to the airport before that plane takes off."

* * *

Luckily the Tallahassee airport wasn't that big, and the Naples airport was even smaller. There were only a handful of airlines with connections in both cities.

It took him the whole three minutes on the phone, but he was sure he'd found the flight she'd taken and he'd managed to get himself a seat on it, as well. Now, he thought, settling into the back seat of the cab, all he had to do was get there before the plane took off.

And then he had to explain what he'd done.

Brian groaned and rubbed his aching head. He had a hangover and a half, an empty stomach, save for the champagne that still seemed to be popping and hissing in there, and he was afraid he'd just ruined a friendship that had endured for twenty years.

How the hell could he explain himself? he wondered. He wasn't even sure what he'd done, although he had a pretty good idea. He'd been making love to one woman in his mind while he held another one in his arms.

And it was unforgivable, especially since he knew the other woman so well.

He kept seeing that uncharacteristically cold look in her eyes this morning, kept seeing the hurt as well. He'd hurt her badly, and he hated the idea of hurting Shelly.

It might not have been so bad, might have even been forgivable, if there hadn't been a time when she'd wanted very much for their relationship to move in that direction. She hadn't been much more than a kid at the time, and she'd never come right out and said anything to him about it, but she'd had an awful crush on him when she was fifteen or sixteen.

Brian had been in college, but he'd spent weekends and summers at home, courting Rebecca, with Shelly watching his every move. He'd remembered that time so clearly this morning when she'd glared at him with the very same look she'd had in her eyes when she was fifteen or sixteen, watching him with Rebecca.

Now he'd hurt her again, worse than he ever had before, and he felt like a louse.

An even worse thought crossed his mind then. What if it wasn't just some sixteen-year-old crush they were dealing with here? What if it was something more recent? More... adult?

That would make things even more complicated, and it made whatever he had done last night even more unforgivable.

Shelly had bit her nails down to the quick by the time the Fasten Seat Belts sign came on and the plane was finally ready to move away from the terminal.

She desperately needed to get out of this town and forget about everything that had happened. She would have been gone last night, except she didn't know where to go or how to get there.

Her money, her credit cards and her keys were in her purse at the bottom of that river.

A purse, she thought. Why did women have to carry purses? Why couldn't they carry a billfold and keys in their pockets, like men did? Like Brian had?

If she had done that, she'd have been able to get away hours earlier. Instead, she'd had to wait at the hotel—like those desperately grateful people in credit-card commercials—for someone to deliver a new card to her so she could get some cash for the ride to the airport, charge a plane ticket and get out of town. She probably should count herself lucky that the card had finally arrived when she'd fled from the hotel room.

The plane's engines revved up, and she relaxed a little. They'd be away from the gate in seconds. Maybe then she could really calm down, knowing she'd escaped, that she'd have at least until Monday morning before she had to face Brian again.

How was she ever going to do that?

She just didn't know. She couldn't imagine. And it wouldn't get any better. Even if she made it that critical first day, what about the next day, the next week, the next month?

She turned back from the window as she heard some sort of commotion in the front of the plane.

Someone was getting on the plane. She heard the flight attendant joking with the person about barely making it in time. And the next thing she knew, her mouth was hanging open, as it had tended to do this past week, and her blood turned cold.

Brian Sandelle was strolling down the aisle.

Shelly couldn't do anything for a few precious seconds. She sat there, frozen in her seat, her eyes drinking in the very sight of him while, at the same time, that crack in her heart seemed to wrench open another centimeter or two.

Vaguely, she thought about trying to hide somewhere, about trying to curl herself into a little ball in the corner and press her face against the window. But it was a foolish thought. It wasn't worth the effort it would take to snap out of this awful, paralyzing shock that had come over her and move those few, precious inches.

He knew she was here.

He'd somehow followed her to the airport and onto this plane, and now she'd be stuck in the air with him until they got to Miami and boarded the short commuter flight to Naples.

Dammit, Shelly cursed under her breath as he paused at the row of seats in front of her and looked at his ticket.

"Fourteen B?" he said, looking from the paper in his hand to the label on the row of seats in which Shelly sat.

She didn't have to look at anything. She already knew; she was in fourteen A.

Shelly turned her face to the window and let her forehead rest against the heavy plastic pane. It was cool to the touch, and her face was flaming.

He was sitting right beside her, she realized miserably. There were three seats in this row and no one sitting in the other two. He could have taken the third seat and left one empty between them, but he didn't.

He sat right beside her, his shoulders a little too broad for the narrow airline seat. Instinctively she found herself drawing inward, her arms and her shoulders hunched together toward the window as she tried in vain not to touch him with any part of her body.

Not that it mattered, she thought as the plane finally pulled away from the terminal and began to taxi. She didn't have to touch him to feel his presence beside her. Her skin was hot to the touch; it felt ultrasensitive in the cool silk of the pretty blouse his mother had brought her yesterday. And her cheeks still stung a little from the unfamiliar feel of a man's face, rough with nighttime stubble, pressed against hers.

She shivered with regrets, her eyes burning with unshed tears at the all-too-clear memory.

"Cold?" he asked, his voice low and so familiar. It sent another shiver down her spine.

He moved beside her, to put his arm around her, she thought, and she made a fool of herself by scrambling to get a little farther away from him. Actually he was doing nothing more than closing the little overhead air-condition nozzle for her.

Shelly felt like an idiot, for the hundredth time or more in less than twelve hours. She'd given away more with that little movement than a thousand words could have told him.

He didn't know anything for sure, Shelly reminded herself. He couldn't remember, and he wouldn't know anything more than what she told him with her words and her body.

"I have to talk to you, Shel."

"No, you don't," she shot back.

He swore, and she flinched at the anger that dripped from the harsh words. Then he took a deep breath and tried again.

"Come on, squirt. Let me say it."

There, Brian thought. That got her head back up and her eyes on him. He'd needed to see her face very badly to push her like this. He needed to know, and now he did.

She almost seemed to hate him in the instant that silly childhood nickname had passed his lips. The possibility of Shelly hating him was the hardest thing he'd had to face in a long time.

He could still see the bruises on the side of her face, where it had banged against the side of the plane. He could still remember how it had felt to hold her on the riverbank and think about what it would have felt like to lose her. He thought of how selfish he'd been to ask her to come with him on this trip and get her involved in this whole ugly scene.

He thought of how unfair he'd been to her.

He wondered how all the feelings he'd ever had for her, the ones he'd taken for granted, that he'd never given a second thought to, could have gotten this tangled up inside him at this moment. And God help him, he couldn't help but think of all the things he'd done to her in his mind, in that incredible dream, and he wondered how many of them had been real.

How many of them could have been real without him realizing it?

She was so much shorter than Rebecca, he thought as he looked her over from head to toe, sitting in her seat beside him. She was so much slighter, her figure almost boyish. She should have felt so different in his arms. That alone should have told him something was wrong last night.

He closed his eyes and tried to remember. Exactly how had the dream woman felt in his arms? How had her body fit with his? How had it felt to slip inside her...?

Brian swore again as his body made it all too clear that it remembered, even if his brain was still foggy on some of the most important details. He shifted uncomfortably in the too-small seat and tried to find a position in which it wouldn't be so obvious that a certain part of his body was straining against the material of the old jeans his mother had dug out of the closet.

The captain came over the intercom then, telling them they were next in line for takeoff and warning them of some turbulence between here and Miami. Immediately the engines started whining and straining against themselves, until the captain let the plane shoot forward on the runway.

The plane lifted off the ground, roaring into the skies. Shelly kept a white-knuckled grip on the armrest between them, and Brian felt like a jerk.

Just what she needed, he thought, another plane ride, two days after their crash, turbulence in the air between here and Miami and him in the seat beside her. He figured the nicest thing he could do for her right now was to somehow distract her while the plane climbed into the sky, and he knew two surefire topics of conversation that could do it.

The night before or the day before that? He pondered over the choices, then decided that she'd probably take a conversation about the plane crash better than the other one.

"The phone call I got when you left," he said, not giving her a chance to cut him off. "It was from the FAA inspector who's handling the crash."

She looked straight ahead, and she didn't move a muscle.

"The guy said the emergency crew got the plane out of the river late yesterday, and he spent most of the night going over it.

"Shelly, there's no easy way to say this. The guy said it's too soon to tell for sure, but I know how these people work. They're very careful and very cautious about releasing any information on a crash until they're sure what happened, but..."

"What?" she demanded.

"The guy said he felt as if he had to warn us. He believes someone tampered with the plane. He thinks someone tried to kill us."

She looked at him then, finally. "That's crazy," she said. "Why would anyone want to kill us?"

"I don't think they did," Brian said. "We weren't even supposed to be on the plane. No one but Charlie knew we would be using it, until I called the hangar Thursday and told them we'd be taking the plane for the weekend."

"So what's going on?"

Brian shook his head. "The only thing I know is that Charlie was supposed to be flying to Saint Petersburg on Monday on business. I don't know who else knows that, and I don't know why anyone would want to hurt him. Do you?"

She hesitated for a full three seconds, then said, "No."

"What?" Brian said, jumping into the silence she'd left. "You know something?"

"Nothing," she insisted. "I'm sure it's nothing."

"Let me be the judge of that," he said.

"I just..." She shook her head back and forth, obviously having trouble taking it all in. "I got this phone call last week."

"Go on," he urged.

"A man, one who wouldn't tell me his name."

"What did he say?"

"That I had to get away from the engineering firm. That there was danger there."

"What kind of danger?"

"The man didn't say. He just wanted me to get out of there for some reason. He said it was too dangerous in that office for me to stay there."

That brought up a lot of questions in his mind—about the business and the reputations of the people they worked with and the kinds of danger the man could have possibly been referring to. But that wasn't what he asked first.

The first thing he worried about was her—her safety and her reasons for not sharing it with him.

"Why the hell didn't you tell me?" Brian asked, too harshly. He realized it the instant the words left his mouth.

"Why would I?" she shot right back at him. "I'm not a little girl anymore. I don't need a keeper. I'm all grown up now."

"I noticed," he said before he could stop himself, managing all too well to turn the conversation to the one she'd been dreading.

Shelly blushed furiously. And Brian was sure she spent more than a moment considering the merits of slapping his face. He was relieved when she didn't, although he would have argued that he probably deserved it. And he hated this awkwardness between them, the one he'd put there through his own stupidity.

"I'm sorry," he said, backing off as best he could. "Really, I am. And I know that you don't want to talk about this, but I think we have to, Shel. Tell me what happened last night."

"Nothing," she said, closing her eyes so he couldn't see anything that they might give away. "Nothing happened."

"Like hell it didn't," he said. The dream was much too vivid for him to believe that.

He looked her over one more time, looking past the bruises on her face and the guarded look in her eyes. He remembered the way she'd flinched earlier when she thought he was going to touch her, as if she couldn't stand to have him near her.

Appalled at himself, Brian wondered if he'd hurt her last night. Sex could be such a physical thing, and he was a big man. He'd always taken care never to hurt a woman, but who could say what kind of care he'd taken last night? She was such a tiny thing. It wouldn't take much to hurt her, he thought.

What in the world had he done to her? He just didn't know, and it was all he could do to keep himself from leaning closer to her, from drawing in the scent of her. He wanted to know if it matched the one he remembered when he was in the shower this morning, when he would have sworn he was washing the distinctive scent of a woman off his skin.

"There was nothing to it," she insisted. "It was a silly misunderstanding."

"It was more than that," he said, just as insistent. He was sure of that. Her reaction told him clearly.

"Brian," she almost pleaded with him. "You were drunk. You'd just watched the woman you love marry someone else and—"

"What? What else?"

"Nothing else."

"Then why are you so upset? Why were you trying to run away from me this morning?"

She shifted in her seat, bringing herself another inch or two farther away from him, and knitted her fingers together with her hands in her lap while she considered her words very carefully. "I just wanted to go home," she said, her knuckles turning white. "That's all. Look at everything that's happened this weekend and surely you can understand that. I just wanted to go home."

He wasn't buying it for a second. Not one single, solitary second. But he thought he'd seen the glisten of tears in her eyes, too, and he'd feel like even more of a heel than he already did if he pushed her so hard he made her cry. There'd be time to get to the bottom of this, time to try to make amends, if he could somehow do that, once they got back to Naples.

"Shelly," he said, totally at a loss as to what he could possibly do now, but unable to ignore the need inside him to somehow ease her pain.

"Please, just leave it alone," she pleaded softly as the bottom seemed to fall out from under the plane.

It seemed to drop a good three inches, then whip back up again, drawing gasps from the first-class section to the tail.

Shelly put one her hand over her mouth and the other around her waist.

"You going to be okay?" Brian asked, touching her lightly, easily, without even thinking about it.

"Don't." She flinched as if he'd struck her, then tried to soften it with softer words this time. "Please don't."

He took a deep breath, then let it out as he tried to assess the situation.

He didn't think she'd let him touch her again, and he couldn't say that he blamed her. He also didn't think he could be this close to her and keep from touching her, not when she so obviously needed comfort. Fighting himself every inch of the way, Brian did all he could. He made himself move into the aisle seat, leaving an empty one in between them.

He figured she'd appreciate even that small distance, and he wasn't willing to go any farther, not just yet, not until he'd decided what to do.

If any other man had hurt her this way, he'd have wrung the guy's neck. But he'd done this himself. And he didn't see how he could ever make it up to her.

Brian sat rigid in the seat, staring straight ahead, smelling again that heady womanly smell, hearing again the music of that slow, sexy saxophone they'd danced to the night before.

It was a rough flight. They'd run into some serious thunderstorms, and after about fifteen minutes of watching Shelly fight her own fears, Brian had had all he could stand. He moved back over into the seat he'd vacated earlier, pushed the armrest up and into the space between his and Shelly's seats and hauled her already trembling body into his arms.

"Don't push me away," he said.

Shelly felt something inside her turning to mush at the sound of his voice and the feel of him as his arms closed around her. She couldn't fight him right now. Her self-protective instincts were as strong as anyone's, but she was exhausted and frightened and furious, all at the same time. And she just couldn't fight him anymore.

Last night had been a nightmare—dancing with him, kissing him, letting him see how she felt about him, only to find out that she'd been mistaken for his precious Rebecca.

She'd been absolutely, totally humiliated. And this was the last time he was ever going to do this to her, she vowed, even as the plane lurched again and he pressed her head against his chest, so close she could hear his heartbeat beneath her ear.

Last night was the last time she was ever going to allow herself to be made a fool of over Brian Sandelle, she promised herself, even as she clung to him.

She still loved him. Maybe she always would. Maybe that was just going to be a fact of life for her. But that didn't mean she could stand to waste another day of her life waiting for him to love her back.

It wasn't going to happen.

If it hadn't by now, it never would.

"Ahh," she called out as the thunder crackled overhead and the plane swayed sickeningly on the wind.

"It's going to be okay," Brian said, leaning down toward her. He turned her face up to his, leaving his hand flush against her cheek. His eyes locked on hers, and she found her lips no more than three or four inches from his, found her breath mingling with his.

"I promise," he said. "I'll made it right again." And he wasn't talking about the sickening plane ride they were on.

What was she going to do now? What was she going to do about these feelings she had for him, now that he'd made it so clear there was only one woman in his heart, that there probably would never be room for more than the one who was already there? She looked up at him and tried to remember her vow not to cry over him ever again.

"Do you know how much I hate the idea of hurting you?" Brian asked huskily, and it cut to the quick, as if he'd laid open her chest in one stroke and bared her heart to him.

"Yes," she said. She did know that he felt something for her. It just wasn't at all what she wanted him to feel; it wasn't nearly enough. And she couldn't make him feel what she wanted him to feel for her.

She couldn't make him love her.

Chapter 7

Monday morning, not yet daylight, and Shelly was sure it was going to be a rotten day because she was about to come face-to-face with Brian again, mere hours after she'd gotten rid of him.

He was driving her to work. He'd insisted, and by the time she'd finally gotten home Sunday, she'd been too tired to argue with the man and too eager to escape from him to bother to try to talk him out of it. It had been a foolish move—short-term relief for long-term trouble. But she'd been desperate yesterday. Today she'd pay for it.

Tonight she'd start looking for a new job, one that would take her far, far away from Brian Sandelle.

She couldn't stand to have her stomach tied into knots every day when she went to work simply because he was there.

Shelly was bone tired, still stiff and sore from the plane crash, still humiliated by what had happened after the wedding, still puzzled by what the FAA inspector had told Brian.

And there were a dozen little irritating things that she had to take care of, things that were complicating her life now when she was ill equipped to cope with them. Her keys were gone, so she couldn't drive her car until she went to the dealer today and got a new set. She shouldn't drive, anyway, until she replaced her driver's license. She'd had to get the rental manager to let her into her own apartment today and arrange to have new keys made for that lock.

One little thing piled on top of another, until she was ready to scream.

That's when he showed up, the man she'd been dreading seeing, here at her apartment at six-fifteen in the morning. There was no justice in the world, she decided.

"Hi," he said as he got out and opened the car door for her, catching her totally unaware of the dangers in such a move.

Her body brushing past his ever so lightly as she got into the car, the feel of him next to her bringing every detail of the night before last and the treacherous morning after it to mind.

Shelly tried not to let Brian see how much it bothered her to have him touch her in this small way, even as she vowed to remember not to give him another opportunity to help her in and out of a car.

"Hi," she finally managed to say.

He got in behind the wheel. She was fooling with the unfamiliar seat belt, trying to get it fastened, so she didn't see the hand that came up to her face, the fingers curling around her chin to turn it gently toward him. "How's the head?"

"Still hurts," she said as he took the opportunity to study her more closely than she would have liked.

"It looks like hell," he said, one finger tracing the outline of the bruise, one she hadn't been able to cover, even with a ton of makeup.

Shelly made herself endure this small touch without her breath catching in her throat. It was a good test for her, she decided. How much could she stand? She'd need to know her limits if she was going to get through the next few weeks, maybe even months, before she could line up a new job.

Brian didn't know anything for sure, she reminded herself, nothing but what she told him and what she showed him with her own responses to him. She'd shown him much too much yesterday. She couldn't show him anything more.

"You sleep okay?" he asked, finally taking his hand away.

"Like the dead," she lied, then changed the subject. "Did you talk to Charlie yet?"

"I couldn't get him yesterday," he said, starting the car and pulling into the almost empty street. "But I left a message on his machine and asked him to meet us at the office, early. Maybe we can clear this up before everybody else gets there."

Shelly nodded. She still found it hard to believe that anyone would deliberately try to hurt Charlie Williams. The man had been like a substitute father to her ever since she'd come to work for him when she'd graduated from engineering school. He and his wife, Marion, had lost their daughter in an automobile accident when she was a teenager, and if she'd lived, she and Shelly would have been the same age.

Charlie hadn't just given Shelly a job; he and his wife had sort of adopted her. They'd been lonely, and Shelly, in a strange town and starting a new job, had been lonely, too. She trusted Charlie. She'd never doubted him, until that strange conversation she'd had with him last week about the even stranger phone call she'd gotten at the office.

She hadn't told Brian about it because she'd wanted a chance to go through it again by herself.

She'd talked to Charlie Monday afternoon, after she'd so foolishly agreed to go to the wedding with Brian. Charlie had insisted that nothing strange or mysterious was going on at the firm and that she had no cause to worry.

He was sure the call was nothing more than a prank.

Shelly hadn't believed a word he'd said to her, but she didn't think Charlie had ever lied to her before.

If she hadn't had so many other things on her mind, she'd have gotten to the bottom of that right then and there. But the day had brought one surprise after another, none of them pleasant. Could the phone call be connected to whatever happened to the plane?

It was hard to believe, but she wondered if it could.

Charlie Williams got to the office around seven, and he looked bad.

He wasn't a handsome man, by any means. He was short, rounded and balding, with a kind face and an affection for smelly cigars. Charlie pulled one out as he settled himself into the big leather chair behind his desk that morning.

"You all right?" he asked gruffly, looking at the big bruise on Shelly's face.

She nodded, watching his face, as well. He looked awful, worse than he had three and a half years ago when he'd finally given in and put his wife, who suffered from Alzheimer's disease, in a nursing home. He seemed to wither up, inside and out, after that, to shrink inside himself. He'd seemed almost frail for a while. Shelly thought he looked that way again now.

"What happened?" Charlie asked, looking to Brian to explain.

"We were almost to Tallahassee when the engine went out. We're damned lucky to be alive."

Charlie shook his head. He fidgeted in his seat and tapped the end of the cigar on the surface of the desk. "What went wrong?"

"I don't know. The FAA inspector's focusing on some sort of problem with the oil line, maybe the oil supply, though he's not sure if he'll be able to check it. The oil case was broken when they hauled the plane out of the river, so whatever was in there is mixed with the water now."

"The gauge?" Charlie asked, a man of few words.

"It didn't show anything until the engine quit," Brian said.

"That's it?"

"That's all I know, except that the FAA inspector thinks someone tampered with it. He thinks someone tried to kill us." Brian seemed to be deliberately challenging him, and Shelly wondered why he was being so harsh about it until she looked back to her boss.

Charlie Williams, a man with an almost ruddy complexion, was nearly white, and he refused to meet her eyes.

Shelly felt a nasty chill work its way down her spine. Her brain was telling her something her heart was having trouble accepting. She couldn't believe Charlie would ever knowingly put her in danger, and yet, from the way he was reacting now, she'd swear that he knew what this plane crash was all about.

"This inspector—he's sure about this?" Charlie asked.

"No," Brian admitted. "But it's his gut reaction. And the man says he's been in the business for fifteen years."

Charlie didn't say anything for the longest time. He just fidgeted with his cigar.

Shelly looked from one man to the other as the tension swirled between them. She trusted them both. She'd known them both for years, and she didn't like being caught between the two of them like this.

"You know why this happened." Brian broke the stalemate with a statement rather than a question.

"No," Charlie said, too quickly.

"You have some ideas," Brian challenged him.

Charlie hedged for all he was worth, but Brian wouldn't have it.

"It's your plane, and you were supposed to take off in it today to go to Saint Pete," Brian said. "It had to be aimed at you, not us."

"Oh, come on," Charlie said, rallying now. "This sounds like something out of a bad TV movie. Why would anybody want to kill me?"

"I don't know," Brian said. *But you do.*

Shelly could almost hear him say it aloud, and she couldn't believe what was happening in this office.

Brian finally gave up and settled back into his chair. Charlie puffed on his cigar, and Shelly tried to take it all in.

"He was lying," Brian said once they'd closed themselves up in his office.

"I can't believe that," Shelly said, sitting down in the chair opposite his desk, then leaning back in the seat. She was exhausted, and her workday hadn't even started. "Why would he lie to us?"

"You tell me. You've known him a lot longer than I have."

"I don't know."

"Business trouble?" he suggested.

"Not now. Not that I know of. He was having a lot of problems five or six years ago from what I've heard from some of the other people in the office."

"Why?" he asked, all business.

Shelly would gladly discuss business with him all day, as long as they could keep away from anything remotely personal.

"Mostly because he was spending so much time away from the office," she explained. "His wife was ill, with Alzheimer's disease. He tried for a long time to take care of her at home, but it got to be too much for him and too dangerous for her. She needed someone watching over her twenty-four hours a day, for her own safety, and Charlie couldn't manage that."

Shelly could easily see how the firm could have been in trouble then. It was a small office, and it was too much Charlie's baby to get along without him for long. He'd been in business in this town forever; he had the connections that brought in the business. Those people also tended to want his personal touch on the jobs they gave him.

She was sure it had been rough around here without him, but she was sure the business was coming out of that now.

"So what did he do?" Brian asked.

"He put Marion in a nursing home right after I came to work here, and once he got her settled, he didn't do much of anything but work. He turned the business back around."

"Well," Brian considered. "If the business is sound, what about his personal life? Gambling? Drinking? Drugs? Women?"

Shelly shook her head to all four. "He's a good man, Brian. You know that."

"I think he is, but something's going on around here. You saw how he was in there."

Yes, she had, and it had her more worried about Charlie than scared for herself. The man meant a great deal to her. He was a mentor, as well as a good friend.

"He seemed so scared," she said.

"Well, he ought to be. Somebody's trying to kill him, and they missed and almost got us instead."

"Do you really believe that?" Shelly said.

"I'm careful up there. I checked that plane myself before we took off. It was fine."

"So what could have happened?"

"I don't know, but I'm going to find out. I want to know why our boss has started lying to us, too," Brian said. "Think about it, Shel. What kind of trouble could he be in?"

She could only shake her head. She dreaded telling Brian what else she knew, but, in fairness, she felt she had to tell him. She'd started to, on the plane, but they'd gotten side-tracked about the night before, and she never got around to finishing the discussion about the strange phone call.

"None of this makes any sense to me," she told him, "but there's something about that phone call I got last week...."

"The one you told me about?"

"Yes.... I think I know the man. I'm almost sure I've heard his voice before."

"You didn't tell me that part."

Shelly decided the best thing to do was to avoid that question altogether, so she just continued. "Something else . . . he knew me. He knew my voice. That's what scared me so much about it—that he knew me."

Brian swore softly for a minute, then turned back to her. "It was Monday morning, when you almost hit me over the head with the paperweight? Wasn't it?"

"Yes."

"I was right there, and you didn't even tell me about it?"

"I thought it was just a silly prank. I mean, it was ridiculous—some vague warning about danger in this office. I know these people, Brian. I've worked with them for years. They're good people."

"Maybe so, but you don't know who could be after them," he said. "It's a crazy world out there, Shel. Just look at the evening news."

"I know," she admitted.

"You should have told me," he said, seeming almost to be hurt by the fact that she hadn't. "You should have trusted me."

"I do."

"Even after this weekend?"

Shelly turned away, hopefully too quickly for him to see the color flooding her cheeks. She had to get used to this. That night would always be there between them, and she was going to have to deal with it for now. "Of course I trust you."

She heard him moving around in the too-narrow space, saw him coming around the side of the desk to sit on the edge near where she sat.

"Shelly—"

"It was nothing, Brian. Absolutely nothing. Can't we just forget about it?"

"Can you?"

It was her turn to swear, and she hoped he hadn't been reading her lips right then. No, she couldn't forget about it. She wouldn't for a long time to come. But she was going to put it behind her and get on with her life. She'd made a promise to herself that she intended to keep.

"I did tell someone about the phone call," she said, shifting the conversation to something she knew could hold his attention. "I told Charlie."

"What did he say?"

Shelly tried to remember his exact words, but couldn't. "Just that he didn't know what the guy could have been talking about."

"What else?" Brian demanded. "What else didn't you tell me the first time?"

"I didn't believe him," Shelly said. "I didn't believe him for a second. Not now and not then."

Chapter 8

Shelly hit the trade journals that night, scanning the advertisements for job openings.

She should have done this as soon as Brian started to work in her office, but she'd thought she could handle it. She'd thought she'd come so much farther than she had in putting her feelings for him firmly in the past.

Obviously she'd been fooling herself, and she couldn't do that anymore.

Shelly sipped a cup of hot chocolate while she scanned the ads, starting with the ones from west coast firms. If she was going to go, she might as well go all out. Seattle sounded good to her. Maybe Portland, if she could stand the cold.

She was going to do it this time, she promised herself. She was going to put him out of her mind and out of her heart. She was going to—

The doorbell rang, startling her as the noise broke the stillness of her apartment.

She glanced at the clock—nearly eleven—and wondered who could be coming to see her at this hour. Then she remembered the phone call from last week, the problem with the plane.

Danger, the man had said. She still had trouble believing she was in danger.

Cautiously she peered through the peephole in the door and, for an instant, she was relieved when she saw who it was. For no more than an instant, that is.

"Brian?" she said, opening the door, then shivering in the cool air that swirled in.

Too late, she realized what she was wearing—a well-worn, plain cotton man's dress shirt with tails that hung to her knees in front and back, but dipped higher on the sides.

"What's wrong?" she asked, when he didn't say anything.

He just stood there in the doorway, looking at her. He made a bad habit of that lately. Shelly fought the urge to button one more button of her shirt, and she wished she'd left on her bra.

"I was out driving," he finally said. "Couldn't sleep. I was wondering . . . can I come in?"

Her instincts said no—a thousand times no. "It's late," she said.

"I won't stay long."

She thought he would have shouldered his way past her, but she backed out of his way first, then realized she'd let him into her apartment, late at night, with her in nothing but a shirt and her panties.

She couldn't win, she decided.

Brian stood in the entranceway with his hands in his pockets, searching his brain for the half-dozen excuses he'd come up with for being here at this time of night.

He couldn't remember one, though. He didn't think she'd appreciate hearing the truth—that he was about to go crazy worrying about her. Some idiot was trying to kill their boss, some man on the phone thought it was too dangerous for Shelly to even be in the office and she didn't trust him enough to tell him about the whole thing. He'd thought of all those things while he tried to talk himself out of coming over here. But now that he'd arrived, he just stood there, staring at her in that shirt.

Something in his normally methodical, meticulous brain seemed to have short-circuited in the past week. He seemed to be incapable of logical thought—otherwise, he never would have found himself in this position. Otherwise, he'd be thinking of a way to get out of it, instead of doing what he was doing—staring at her in that damned shirt.

He'd told her on the plane ride home yesterday that he knew she wasn't a little girl anymore, but maybe he hadn't realized that. He sure hadn't taken a good look at her lately, not like this, anyway.

He started to loosen his tie, then realized he wasn't wearing one. The tightness in his throat was coming from some other source, and he was staring at the problem right now.

She had grown up. She was still pint-size, but then she probably always would be. He figured she was maybe five foot two. But she had these incredible legs halfway hidden under those shirttails. And the scrawny kid he'd remembered so well was still thin, but the curves were there, too, in all the right places.

He'd bet a month's salary that she wasn't wearing a bra; he could tell by the way her breasts swayed under the shirt while she moved. And he could only hope that she had anything at all on under that shirt.

"Brian?" she said, her cheeks flushed.

She was either angry or embarrassed by the way he'd been looking her over. He couldn't tell which. And then something else—something that made him decidedly uneasy—occurred to him.

"Are you alone?" he asked, a little too harshly, too demandingly. He had this sudden interest in finding out what had happened to the man who belonged to that shirt.

"What?" she said.

"The shirt?" He knew he was in trouble, but it was too late to stop. And he wanted to know where she'd gotten the damned shirt. "It's a man's shirt."

She folded her arms across her chest and the ends of the shirt gaped open another inch, surely not what she intended when she crossed her arms, but that was the net effect.

"Yes," she admitted. "It is." And then she waited, not giving an inch, making him go ahead and say what he had no business saying.

"Well, whose shirt is it?"

"I don't remember," she shot back at him.

A few years ago, he would have expected something like that from her. She'd been full of sass as a teenager. He would have laughed a few years ago.

Instead, he swore out loud. He didn't think it was funny now. He didn't see anything funny about the whole situation.

And he couldn't remember what she looked like underneath that shirt, although, when he closed his eyes and went back to that night, he thought he could remember what she felt like, beneath those clothes.

She was lying about the shirt, he decided in a moment when logic prevailed. She wasn't the kind of woman who'd have a parade of men coming through her bedroom and leaving pieces of clothing behind.

He wondered what the man meant to her, wondered if the man whose shirt she wore had hurt her as he had himself. And Brian wondered how badly he'd hurt her, even as he scanned the apartment for any telltale signs that she wasn't alone.

Two glasses? Two dinner plates? A jacket that looked too big for her to wear? He didn't see any of those things, but he felt only marginally better.

"Is he still here?" Brian asked, unable to stop himself from heading down this treacherous road. He was determined to know if he'd interrupted anything, if someone had been waiting for her to get back from Tallahassee.

"Who?" she asked.

"The man who belongs to that shirt."

"Oh, for God's sake, we're alone, okay? Are you satisfied now? This is my shirt. I sleep in it. It's big and it's comfortable. It's none of your business, but if you must know, the man who used to own it has been out of my life for a long time." She placed her hands on her hips while she put him in his place, and the shirt ends shifted enticingly along her neck and her collarbone.

Brian helped it along on her right side, uncovering a distinctive, reddish mark at the base of her throat.

"Then I guess I must have been the man who left this on you," he said, still unable to help himself as his fingers traced the small circle of darkened skin, a mark of passion.

"Damn you!" she said, flinching away from his touch, but standing her ground. "What is it about men? Your caveman ancestry? You don't want me for yourself, but you don't like the idea of anyone else having me, either?" Shelly hated herself for admitting that to him, hated him a little for pushing her into saying it.

What did the man want from her, after all? What could he want that she hadn't already given him?

"Shel—"

"Get out, Brian. Get out of here now."

For a minute, she didn't think he was going to leave. She glared at him, daring him not to, while she pulled the ends of her shirt back together.

"Shelly, I swear, I never meant to—"

The phone rang, and she was never so grateful to hear that sound.

"Go!" she told him as she turned to answer it.

A man's voice, muffled in a curious way, came to her through the phone. "I heard there was some trouble with the plane," he told her.

It was him again—the man who'd called the office the week before—and he knew where she lived.

Shelly whirled around and was grateful to see that Brian hadn't walked out the door yet.

This man on the phone knew where she lived. She shivered at the thought.

Brian must have seen that she was upset, because he closed the door behind him and walked back into the room.

She turned her back to him and spoke softly into the phone. "Who is this? If you're really trying to help me, then you'll tell me who you are and what you know."

"I can't," the man said. "It wouldn't do you any good, and if you said anything to the wrong person, it might get me killed."

Shelly didn't say anything for a moment. She didn't see how she could. Brian was too close, and she could just imagine how he'd react to this phone call. She might never get rid of him tonight if he knew who was on the other line.

"Shelly?" the man on the phone said. "Damn, woman, I'm trying to help you. Can't you understand that? You're in danger there. You have to get out." The man was agitated toward the end, and while he was careful to disguise his voice, he forgot about his own particular choice of words.

Damn, woman. If he'd said that to her once, he'd said it a thousand times.

"Shelly," he said impatiently as she figured it out. "Listen to me this time. Get out. You may not get another chance to get away." And then the phone was buzzing in her ear, the call disconnected from his end.

But it didn't matter that much. She knew who it was. She'd been right. She had known his voice.

"Who was that?" Brian asked, taking the phone from her hand.

"You don't know him," Shelly said, still having a hard time herself believing who it was.

"It was that man again, wasn't it? The one who tried to warn you away from the office last week? What did he say to you? Did he threaten you?"

"No," she said, arguing with herself about what to do next. "It wasn't like that."

"Then who was it?" Brian demanded.

And then Shelly knew exactly what she was going to do and how she was going to accomplish it.

She wanted to be alone tonight, to figure this out as best she could. And once she had some time to herself to think about it, she'd probably tell Brian everything, because she did trust him and she did worry that they both were in danger.

But for now, she just wanted him out of here. She wanted to put her clothes on, put her feet up, lock her doors and try to make sense of it all.

And she knew just how to get Brian to leave her alone without him putting up a fight, without making him suspicious about the call and without lying to him.

"Who was it?" he asked, coming toward her now.

Shelly absolutely stopped him in his tracks. "It was the man who gave me this shirt."

Grant Edwards had been Charlie Williams's second-in-command at the engineering firm when Shelly started working there. They'd dated briefly, casually, after she first came to Naples. He'd helped her paint her apartment one weekend, and he'd brought along a couple of old shirts for them to wear while they did it.

Shelly still wore the shirt around the house sometimes, only because she found it incredibly comfortable. She didn't see any need to explain that to Brian.

She also had no intention of explaining that Grant had been one of a handful of men who Shelly hoped would help her forget all about Brian Sandelle. He'd failed miserably at that. But then so had all the others, Shelly reminded herself as she sat in her darkened apartment, sipping hot chocolate and waiting for the dawn.

One thing, though, if anyone besides Charlie was in a position to know what was going on there, it was Grant.

Grant knew more than anyone did about the business, except for Charlie. If Grant thought she was in a dangerous situation, if he was as scared and desperate as he sounded on the phone, then it must be a very serious situation, indeed.

Shelly thought about that. She thought about the way Charlie had reacted when they'd told him about the plane and how it had felt to watch it fall through the sky.

What in the world was going on here? Her nice, sane world had been turned upside down, and she didn't even know why.

Chapter 9

Two days later and Brian Sandelle was still feeling decidedly uncivilized. He hadn't slept well, and he hadn't figured out a damned thing.

He could have stood that. It was the wondering he couldn't take. He wanted to know whether the man with the light blue dress shirt had shown up at Shelly's after he'd left the other night.

An almost insane reaction—he knew that. A caveman, she'd called him, and he felt rather barbaric this morning. She wasn't his—not in that way. She was a good friend, probably the best female friend he'd ever had, and he was just worried about her, he reasoned with himself.

He was allowed to worry over a good friend caught in the middle of a dangerous situation.

But he shouldn't lose sleep at night, wondering if the man who gave her that shirt was peeling it off of her at that very moment. And it shouldn't bring out some latent caveman tendencies in him.

"You don't want me for yourself," she'd told him. Interesting. He'd never really thought of her that way, but he'd been the one who'd put that mark on her neck.

He shifted back in his chair and gave up on all pretense of working. This was crazy. This was Shelly. This was the girl he'd—

Someone knocked on the door to his office.

"Yes," he said, trying not to let the irritation at the interruption show in his voice. It wasn't like him to be such a bear. It wasn't like him to get drunk, pop some pills and make love on the floor to a woman he'd known forever, either.

"Have you heard from Charlie this morning?" Charlie's secretary, Maureen, asked.

"No. Why?"

"It's almost ten, and he hasn't come in yet."

"I haven't seen him," Brian said. He hadn't seen anybody. He'd come to work a little before seven, closeted himself in his office and tried not to come out. He didn't want to inflict his bad temper on anyone unless he absolutely had to.

"Wait a minute," Brian said as Maureen turned away. "I think his car was in the parking lot when I came in this morning."

Brian had noticed that and thought it was unusual. He normally beat everyone to work in the morning.

"Let's go check," he said, a bad feeling coming over him.

Charlie drove a big tan car that had seen better days. It was sitting in his designated spot. Brian could see it from the window on the east side of the office.

"When did you last see him?" he asked Maureen.

"Yesterday, around lunchtime. He was going to get something to eat, then check on the work at the condominium site near Gulf Shores before heading east of town to do a safety check on a bridge."

"He took one of the company's pickups?" Brian asked.

"I'm not sure, but that's what he usually did when he was going to a construction site." Maureen had this stricken look on her face now. "Do you think something's wrong?"

Brian shrugged, trying to make the movement as nonchalant as possible. "It's not like him to just not show up."

"What should we do?"

"Has anyone else in the office seen or heard from him since noon yesterday?" he asked, heading for Charlie's office.

"I don't know. I haven't asked everyone yet."

"Why don't you do that now?" Brian said. "And call his home number, too."

Brian walked into Charlie's office. He sat down in the man's chair and searched through the stacks of papers that littered the desk until he found Charlie's appointment calendar. He'd had a meeting marked for the hotel site yesterday at two—Brian knew where that was—then the bridge inspection at four, with a highway number, but nothing else to indicate where the bridge might be located.

Maureen came to stand in the door a few minutes later. "No one's heard from him," she said. "And there's no answer at his home."

"Okay," Brian said, not liking the way this sounded at all. "This hotel site isn't more than two miles from here. I'm going to go over there and see if he ever showed up yesterday. Call me on the mobile phone if you hear anything from him."

Maureen nodded, then stepped aside.

For the first time, Brian realized that Shelly was standing behind Maureen. She'd probably heard the whole thing.

"What's going on?" she asked. "What's happened to Charlie?"

It was the first time she'd spoken to him since Monday night when he'd come to her apartment. "We don't know. Nobody's seen him since yesterday."

Brian heard the air leave her lungs in a whoosh. She looked as if she hadn't been sleeping well, either, although that alone didn't mean much, he told himself. She might have been as worried as he was or she might not have been alone.

He remembered the way she'd looked in that shirt—that other man's shirt. He could so easily picture her in that, rather than the long, loose sweater she wore now over those tight knit pants that would have done wonders for her legs if the sweater hadn't hung nearly to her knees. He had no business noticing. He had no time for that, either.

"What are you going to do?" she asked, as he started to move.

"I'm going to find him."

And when he did, he was going to get some answers out of the man.

"What can I do?" she asked.

Brian hated to even tell her what he thought their next step should be, but, as he saw it, it had to be done. If he asked someone else to do it, she'd hear about it soon enough, anyway. The office was too small for secrets to stay secrets for long.

"His car's in the parking lot, so he took one of the company pickups yesterday," Brian said. "Why don't you get the license number and call it in to the police. See if they've found him or the truck."

"Brian?" she said, then couldn't say any more.

The way she said his name seemed to cut right through him, seemed to rip something open inside him. It was like a shot out of the past, from a time when she not only looked up to him but trusted him and depended upon him, as well.

He'd make her trust him again.

"I'll find him, Shel," he said, resisting the urge to touch her.

It didn't take as long as Brian thought it would to find some news. As he was walking through the lobby, the building's security guard flagged him down and pulled him into a conversation with a sheriff's deputy.

"Officer? Brian Sandelle," he said, extending a hand to the older man and trying not to think of what might have happened. "What can I do for you?"

"You're with Williams Engineering?" The man shook his hand.

"Yes, sir."

"You the boss?"

"As close as you're going to get to him today."

The deputy nodded. "We found a white pickup this morning parked on one of the side roads off U.S. 41, about fifteen miles east of town. It had a faded Williams Engineering logo on it."

"We have a couple of trucks like that," Brian said.

The deputy rattled off a license number. "That one of yours?"

"We could go upstairs and check the records," Brian offered, though he already knew it had to be theirs. It was parked on the road that led to the bridge Charlie had gone to inspect. "Did you find anything else?"

"Some ropes—looked like safety lines of some sort—hanging from the bridge."

Brian swore.

"Anyone from your office disappeared?" the deputy said.

"Charlie Williams, the owner, took one of those pickups out yesterday afternoon to inspect a bridge on that road. No one's seen or heard from him since around noon."

"That's, uh, that's bad news."

An understatement if Brian ever heard one. "Did they find anything else?"

"Nothing that anyone's told me about. Does this man have a wife? Kids? We'll need to notify someone."

"Let's go upstairs," Brian said, wondering how in the world he was going to tell Shelly this.

It was unseasonably cold that day and rainy, a perfectly miserable setting for a perfectly awful event.

"I can't believe this is happening," Shelly said as she stood beside Brian on the two-lane bridge.

Brian had been determined to see the bridge where Charlie had disappeared. Shelly had insisted on going, as well. He hadn't liked the idea, but he hadn't wanted to let her out of his sight, either.

The small bridge spanned a normally shallow river that drained into the swamp east of town. With the deputy's permission, Brian inspected the climbing gear, which was at least one knot shy of being effective.

"Charlie was too careful to make an amateurish mistake like that," Shelly said.

"I know," he replied.

Brian stared down at the river, which was running fast as it carried away the runoff from the day-long rain.

"He could have survived the fall," Shelly said, although she didn't sound that convinced of it.

This part of Florida was pretty flat, so it wasn't that much of a fall from the bridge to the river.

"Could have," the deputy with them agreed. "But it's fairly shallow water, and look at those rocks sticking out above the surface over there. He cracks his head on one of those, gets knocked out and he's a goner.''

Yes, Brian agreed, he would have been. If it had happened that way.

"You haven't found anything else?" he asked.

"Not yet," the deputy said. "The truck wasn't locked. It seemed as if he must have been expecting to be coming back in a few moments, else he would have locked it.''

"No sign of a struggle or anything?" Brian said.

The man shook his head. "This is it.''

"Have you searched the river?"

"Not yet. I've got somebody coming to check into it, but I think it's too shallow for us to do that safely—too many rocks out there. We walked the shoreline on either side for about half a mile. Didn't find anything. We'll go farther down river this afternoon if it clears up. If not, we'll hit it tomorrow.''

Shelly shivered in the cool, rain-laden air. "I can't believe this is happening," she said.

She'd taken the news better than Brian had expected, but he suspected she'd just named the reason for that. He was having trouble believing it himself. But the news would sink in eventually, and then . . .

"Shelly." He forced himself to move on, to do what he had to do. "Will you check in with the office, just in case they've heard anything we haven't?"

"Sure," she said.

Brian watched her walk away. It wasn't fifty yards to the side of the road where they'd parked the car, but it was the first time she'd left his side since he'd told her about Charlie.

Brian had one priority that was uppermost in his mind right now—he didn't want her hurt. He didn't know what he was up against, what Charlie was up against, but Brian was going to make damned sure that Shelly didn't get caught in the middle of it.

"Officer?" he said. "You think he's dead?"

Grimly, the uniformed man nodded.

"There are some things you need to know." And Brian proceeded to tell him about the company's plane crashing and Charlie Williams's reaction to it all.

Shelly didn't sleep that night. She spent the hours staring at nothing and trying to figure out why anyone would want Charlie Williams dead. It just didn't make any sense. Nothing did anymore.

They hadn't had any word all day or night, so she was still hopeful. Charlie could have survived that fall. He could be out there somewhere.

She was just getting out of the shower, shortly after dawn, when her doorbell rang.

"Oh, no," Shelly said in the still, empty apartment. She gave herself a minute to lean against the bathroom wall for support before she made her way to the front door.

"Brian?" she said, opening the door to him.

He didn't say anything. He didn't have to. She knew what had happened. "They found his body?"

He nodded.

Charlie, she thought, closing her eyes tight. Gone for good. One more person who'd disappeared from her life. Her mother, her father and now this.

"C'm'ere, Shel," Brian said, holding out his arms to her.

She shook her head, standing her ground for a moment, trying not to think about Charlie. She just couldn't handle it right now. Instead, she concentrated on fighting back her tears and fighting against the memories of all the other times in her life when Brian had been the one to comfort her.

She'd met him soon after her mother died, and he'd been there when she'd lost her father, as well. It had always been him. At times like now, she thought it always would be. How could she fight against something as strong as this mysterious force that lived between them, one that grew only stronger despite her efforts to stop it.

Charlie was dead, she told herself. They'd found his body.

And, as always, Brian was here.

"Oh, Brian," she sobbed.

Wordlessly he closed the distance between them and took her into his arms.

She let herself sag against him, and he caught her fast against his big, powerful body. He'd done this so many times before. But this was different. She'd never felt so vulnerable, so confused, so angry and so scared. He'd never felt so good.

Brian was as solid as a rock, and not just because he was so tall and so strong. He was a man you could depend upon, one you could trust with your life. She had already done that—in the muddy river in Tallahassee where their plane had landed.

She clung to him now, as she had there on that riverbank, and she wondered where they'd found Charlie. She wondered if he'd drowned, as she nearly had, in that murky rain-swollen water. She knew how it had felt. She remembered the panic and the struggle to no avail, and she prayed that what had happened to Charlie had been just what the deputy had suggested. She hoped the rocks got him as he hit the water and he hadn't known anything after that.

Oh, Charlie, she thought, surprised at how much she'd forgotten about the kind of pain that came with losing someone, surprised at how very alone she felt at that moment. More than anything, she wanted to just let herself go, to let herself sob her heart out in Brian's arms, but she made herself pull away from him. It was too easy to hang on to him this way, and she wanted too much to depend upon him.

Shelly hadn't expected Brian to resist, but he did, holding on to her for a moment, as if to ask her if she was sure she wanted to do that. She didn't, but she knew she needed to.

Things had changed between them that night in the hotel, and whether or not she was upset, whether or not she was grieving for a dear friend, she couldn't let herself be held in his arms any longer. Believe it or not, she did have some sense of self-preservation.

He seemed to know it, too—that things had changed between them. And he didn't seem to like it. That was clear, even as he gave in and let her go.

"I'm sorry," he told her. "I know he meant a lot to you."

She nodded, brushing her tears away before he could do it for her.

He would have wiped them away. It wouldn't be the first time he'd done that for her. She wondered if it would be the last. She wondered who she had left to lose.

No one but him. Unless, of course, she admitted that he'd never been hers to lose—not in the way she wanted him, not in the way she needed him.

One more sob got away from her, and Brian took a step closer.

"Shel?" he said. "Let me . . ."

She shook her head.

"Is it just gone?" he said. "All those years of our friendship, everything we shared and all we meant to each other? Is it gone?"

She tried to explain the unexplainable to him, but got out nothing more than a sigh, then a shrug. Finally two little words, totally inadequate to express the myriad feelings she was fighting, came out. "It's different."

He shifted his weight from one foot to the other, swallowed hard and looked as uncomfortable as she felt. "And you can't stand to have me touch you anymore?"

She dropped her eyes to the floor and kept them there. Dear God, she didn't want to have this conversation. What purpose would it serve, anyway? She couldn't think of a one. What could she say to him to explain? Nothing that would make things any better. But she could make it worse, she knew; that was certainly a possibility.

Morosely, she stood before him and contemplated the vanilla-colored tile of the entranceway while she thought of a way to get out of this.

Brian took her hand and tugged gently until she looked at him again, then he let it go.

"I know you don't want to talk about that night, but—"

"No," she said in a rush.

"One thing," he said, his own eyes dropping to the floor. "I have to know."

"Brian, please..."

"Did I hurt you?" he said roughly.

"No," she said, her breath coming out in a rush. She knew the pain he meant was physical. "Not that way."

A woman would definitely be angry for being mistaken for another woman, but it wouldn't hurt her feelings this much unless she cared deeply for the man in question. It wasn't as if she'd told him something he didn't already know.

He had to have known how she felt. She suspected he'd known for years.

What did it really matter to have it all out in the open? She probably couldn't be any more embarrassed than she already was over what had happened that night.

"I'm sorry, Shel. I know that's not nearly enough, but I'm so damned sorry."

"I know," she said.

"I . . . Aw, hell. This isn't the time. I know that."

She nodded. There wasn't ever going to be a time to discuss this, not if she got her wish.

"Look," he said, "somebody has to go to the morgue and identify the body. I can do that. But somebody has to tell his wife, too, and I don't even know which nursing home she's in. One of the deputies will go, if I can tell him where she is, but I thought . . ."

"I'll do it," she said. She couldn't stand the thought of Marion Williams hearing about this from a total stranger, even if the woman was unlikely to comprehend what they told her.

"Thanks," Brian said. "I'll go with you."

Shelly put a hand to her cheek; it was wet, and her hand was shaking. "It just doesn't make any sense."

"I know," Brian said.

"He was a good man."

"I know."

"He wouldn't make a mistake like that with the safety line." She was sure of that. "He didn't fall."

"We'll figure it out," Brian promised her.

And she believed him and found some measure of comfort in his promise.

Chapter 10

Marion Williams didn't understand a thing Shelly tried to tell her. She didn't even know who Shelly was. Marion had thought her long-lost daughter had come back from the grave.

Shelly sat in the passenger seat of Brian's car and watched the rain fall around them, let the misery consume her as they sat in the parking lot. Brian sat beside her, not talking to her, not touching her. But he was with her. He hadn't been willing to let her do this on her own, and she appreciated that.

"How long has she been like that?" he asked.

Shelly shrugged her shoulders and tried to remember when Marion Williams hadn't been like that. "As long as I've known her, she's had days like that. She used to have days where she knew the people around her, she knew who she was and what year it was. Now she's like this most of the time."

Brian started the car and turned on the heater; it was getting chilly in the car. But he didn't make any move to start driving. "Do you think you got through to her?"

"I don't know. I mean, I'm sure that on some level she'll realize that Charlie's gone and wonder where he is. But I don't know if she can comprehend the idea that he's never coming back."

Shelly pulled the ends of her sweater together as she waited for the car to get warm. She wondered if it would ever stop raining. She wondered if Charlie had suffered in the end. She wondered who could have made him so afraid. Who could have made him lie to her? And who could have wanted him dead?

Then she remembered Grant and his strange phone calls. "Oh, God," she said. Grant knew what was wrong. She hadn't thought of it until just now, but he knew.

"Shelly?"

She looked up, finding nothing but the rain running down the foggy windshield. She wondered what it would feel like to let her tears run in big rivulets, like the rain streaming down the safety glass of the windshield.

But she couldn't allow herself to do that. Not yet. Not until she was alone.

"Brian..." She dreaded getting into this with him, but she didn't have any choice. He had taken Grant's place. He was the most senior engineer and second-in-command at the firm. He'd be running things for now.

She had an obligation to tell him, for the sake of the business Charlie was leaving behind, for the safety of everyone who worked in that office.

"There are some things we need to talk about," she said. "The phone calls I got—"

"You got more than one?"

She forgot she hadn't admitted that to him, then remembered the way she'd covered it up. Damn, she thought. Now she'd have to get into her personal relationship with Grant, as well.

"I got another call—"

"The night I was there." His lips stretched into a thin line, a sure sign that he was angry. And he already knew what she'd done. He hadn't asked if it was the call she'd gotten while he was there. He'd simply stated it.

"Yes," she admitted. She risked a glance in his direction and wished that she hadn't.

Why, he asked her, without saying a word. Why had she kept that from him? Why couldn't she trust him, at least where someone's life was at stake?

"Please don't make this any harder than it already is," she said.

Brian threw his hands up in the air in a gesture of surrender, and he didn't say a word.

"He didn't really say anything more than he said the first time, but I recognized his voice this time."

"Who?"

"Grant."

"Edwards? The guy I replaced?"

She nodded.

"Did he have much of a personal relationship with Charlie?"

Shelly considered that for a moment. She knew Charlie fairly well; at least, she thought she had. She didn't remember ever seeing him and Charlie together outside of the office, and neither one had told her anything about any personal interests they had in common.

"I don't know for sure," she said. "I don't think so."

"So whatever the hell is going on with Charlie is most likely work-related, and Edwards found out about it somehow. Don't you think so?"

"I guess. I really didn't remember the call until just now."

"Or this guy could have been part of it," Brian said, thinking out loud. "Where's Edwards now?"

Shelly tried to remember where he'd planned to go after he left Naples fourteen or fifteen months ago. "I'm not sure. He didn't have anything lined up when he left...."

"What did you remember?"

"When he left, he had a big blowup with Charlie. I'd forgotten about it until now. I don't know what it was about, and I couldn't hear what they were saying, but the body language spoke volumes. They were both furious."

Brian nodded. "Edwards figured out what was going on."

"Or Charlie did." She couldn't help but defend him. She couldn't believe Charlie was involved in anything that had gotten him killed. But she couldn't forget how he'd lied to her that day she'd confronted him about Grant's phone call. And she couldn't forget how scared he'd been when she and Brian had told him about the plane crash.

Charlie definitely knew what was going on. He knew he was in trouble, and that, more than anything else, convinced her that he was involved in something he shouldn't have been involved in.

"We'll have to tell the sheriff," Brian said.

"I know."

"Are you up to doing it now?"

No, she wanted to tell him. She didn't want to do anything else, and she wasn't sure she could. But, as she saw it, she didn't have much choice in the matter. It had to be done, and she couldn't leave it to Brian to take care of it for her.

She looked at the rain, still running down the window, and remembered wanting to cry, just like that, the tears running in big streaks down her face. Soon, she promised herself, but not yet.

"I can do it," she told him. "Let's go."

Shelly thought she was going to escape from him relatively unscathed considering all that had happened that day. They'd been to the morgue, the nursing home and the sheriff's department, and she'd handled it all.

She'd spent this whole horrible day with him, from sometime before dawn until after dark, but it wasn't over yet. Somehow he'd invited himself into her apartment after he'd driven her home, and she hadn't figured out how to get rid of him.

Shelly slipped off her shoes, not caring that she barely made it to his shoulder in her stocking feet. She reached down inside herself, desperately searching for some bit of strength she'd held in reserves somewhere.

Clearly the man had something on his mind, and he didn't intend to leave until they'd dealt with it.

Shelly had resigned herself to it, actually. That was how she came to find herself curled up in the corner of the sofa, sipping decaf with him at eight o'clock at night.

"We need to start going through the files at work first thing in the morning," he said.

"I know," she said.

The sheriff hadn't asked them to do that. He hadn't asked much of anything, and he still wasn't convinced that he was dealing with a homicide. Oh, he was suspicious, but he wasn't in a big hurry to investigate why someone had killed Charlie or who that someone might be. He wanted to be sure that someone had actually killed the man first.

Brian didn't need to know any more to convince him to take action. He was sure that what had happened to Charlie was no accident, and he was worried that other people at the office could be in danger. If Charlie's and Grant's only connection was through the office and if both men were aware of the danger they were facing, it stood to reason that there was a good chance the problem was work related.

They were going to search through the records of the jobs both men worked on to see if they found anything suspicious.

"It's still hard for me to believe that some sort of job someone did in that office could have led to a murder," Shelly said.

"Think of the money," Brian said, setting his coffee mug on the table by the couch. "We work on lots of multimillion-dollar jobs."

The firm had changed a great deal since the time Charlie founded it twenty years ago. It had grown tremendously in the time that Naples had seen a building boom, and at one time the office had people specializing in all phases of construction-related engineering work.

But Marion Williams's illness had taken its toll on the business. Charlie had downsized it drastically in order to hang on to it. Charlie had still done a little bit of everything for clients who'd been with him for years. But more and more, the firm had narrowed the scope of its work to civil engineering. They helped design buildings, reviewed construction plans and inspected work to see that those plans were followed.

"People will do anything if enough money's involved," Brian said.

"Some people," she said, still wanting to believe that Charlie hadn't done anything wrong, that he'd merely been caught up in a bad situation he couldn't handle.

Grant could have been doing something—she didn't know what. But it was easier to believe the trouble had started with Grant, and the only thing Charlie had done was to try to stop it.

"I guess I'd better leave if we're going to get an early start." Brian stood. "Do you need a ride tomorrow?"

"No, thanks. My car dealer delivered a new set of keys to the office today." She followed him to the door, retrieving his coat from the closet, all the while thinking she was going to get away without discussing anything personal.

But Brian ended up cornering her at the door.

"This man—this Grant Edwards," he said cautiously, keeping his distance from her. He didn't try to touch her, and she was grateful for that, at least.

"Yes," she said, wishing she'd never met the man. The relationship hadn't lasted long, and it hadn't ended that badly.

Grant hadn't hurt her or frightened her in any way. He'd just left her feeling more alone when she was with him than she had been by herself. He was fairly nice, fairly attractive, more intelligent than most men she'd met, and he'd desperately wanted to go to bed with her.

Shelly had refused, though. He wasn't the man she really wanted. He wasn't the man standing in front of her right now.

She looked up at Brian as he stood in the hallway. He wore jeans and a plain white shirt, a stark contrast to the tan of his skin, with his hair still wet from the rain they'd slogged through all day and his eyes locked on hers.

No, Grant didn't even come close. She'd known that from the beginning, though she'd tried to pretend that it didn't matter.

Shelly finally remembered why she'd come over here—to get his coat for him. She was still holding it in her hands, and she'd forgotten all about it. What must the man think of her? She couldn't imagine.

"Here," she said, finally handing it to him.

"Thanks." He slipped it on, but made no move to leave. "When I was here . . . the other night?"

"Yes."

"You were wearing that shirt." He sounded as reluctant to get into it as she was. "And you said that the man on the phone was the one who'd . . ."

Shelly puzzled over his apparent loss for words. That was unusual and intriguing. "You mean when I said that it was his shirt?" She knew where he was going, and she didn't know how to avoid it, so she figured they might as well get it out in the open. "It was."

He considered that for a moment.

Let him wonder about her and Grant, she decided, if he cared enough to even wonder. He wasn't the only man in her life. Who was she kidding? Brian had never actually been *the* man in her life, only the one in her dreams. She wished he'd stayed there.

"So," he said, having the grace to at least be as uncomfortable as she was. "You and this man . . ."

"What do you want to know, Brian?" she asked, just wanting it over, wanting more than anything to be alone.

He hesitated, and that wasn't like him. Shelly liked the idea that she might have thrown him a little off balance. God knows he'd done it enough to her.

"What was he to you?" he finally asked.

Shelly had no energy left for prevarication, and she was sure Brian had no illusions left about what she felt for him. So she just told him. "Grant was a man I hoped would help me forget about someone else."

She regretted it almost immediately after the words left her mouth, but by then it was too late.

Brian's eyes locked on hers, daring her to look away.

She didn't want him any closer. She didn't want him touching her. So she made herself look at him, and she realized that the man he'd become was even more appealing to her than the boy she'd fallen in love with. Strong, sexy, self-assured. Kind, caring, generous. He was all those things and more. How was she supposed to forget about him? He was rock solid, physically and spiritually. He was the only constant in her life for the past twenty years.

Shelly sighed heavily, seeing no way out for herself. She tried to walk away then, but he stopped her, simply by stepping to the side and blocking her path.

"So," he said softly. "Did he make you forget?"

"No," she said without hesitating, her chin jutting up a fraction as she dared him to ask anything else.

His eyes burned into hers, the intensity leaving her reeling on her feet.

It was all going to come out, she thought. She'd held it in so tightly for years, and she couldn't do it any longer.

The night they'd spent together had ripped through all her carefully constructed barriers and left her completely vulnerable to him. She was exhausted and frustrated and scared. She couldn't escape from this conversation tonight with her secrets intact.

Shelly tried to prepare herself as best she could. She wouldn't cry. She wouldn't try to explain how she'd come to feel what she felt. She wouldn't attempt to justify her emotions to him.

But she didn't have the strength to deny them, either.

She bowed her head and bit back the bitter tears. So easily, they could fall like the rain. It was raining now, enough moisture to feed a million tears.

It seemed as if the whole world was crying tonight.

Brian took a step closer, and she tried to brace herself for what came next. But she miscalculated badly. She'd expected more unwelcome questions, but she got a touch—his lips moving across hers in a kiss that was as soft as the falling rain, and as devastating as anything that had happened to her that day. It was blessedly brief, and it felt like an apology, though she couldn't say for what.

And she wondered if he saw the tears spilling over her tightly closed eyelids before he turned and finally walked out the door.

Chapter 11

The funeral was on Friday, and half the town showed up.
Charlie had lived nearly his whole life there. He was well
known and well liked. He'd be missed, Shelly knew, though
she found little comfort in that thought.

Missed or not, he was gone. One more person had vanished from her life.

Charlie's wife didn't attend the service. Marion's doctor
didn't think she would understand what was going on, anyway, although she did sense that something was wrong.

Shelly stood at the grave site under the funeral-home
canopy, staring at the gleaming brass coffin draped in white
roses, and she felt as if she'd been here a million times before.

She vaguely remembered the days immediately following
her mother's death from ovarian cancer, but her father's
funeral six years before was still so vivid in her mind.

She wondered how many more times in her life she'd
stand at a grave site just like this and say goodbye to some-

one. And then she realized that right now she didn't have anyone left to lose, at least not anyone who was that close to her.

She closed her eyes tightly as she bowed her head and said a quick prayer of her own.

The ceremony was over. It had been for some time, and all the other mourners had drifted toward their cars and started to leave.

Shelly could see the grave diggers standing in the distance, waiting to finish their job once the coffin was lowered into that gaping hole. She clutched the rose she'd taken from the spray of flowers lying on the coffin. She gripped it so hard that one of the thorns bit into her fingertip. Bright red against the pale ivory color of the flower.

It made her a little dizzy to look at it.

That was when Brian finally stepped in, taking the flower from her fingers and wiping a drop of blood from her hand.

She'd known he was there, waiting for her. She could feel the impatience in him as he tried to give her some time alone—he seemed to realize that she desperately wanted to keep her distance from him, and he'd tried to respect her wishes.

But she could feel his eyes on her back as she'd stood there. He'd been beside her during the ceremony, and she couldn't say how she knew, but she was sure he was fighting a battle with himself to keep from touching her.

She was grateful he'd fought it and won for as long as he had. She felt as fragile as that soft white rose he'd thrown to the ground at her feet.

The awkwardness between them—the one she thought might have diminished given the passage of some time—had grown, especially since the other night when she'd all but told him that she'd never been able to forget him, even though he'd never been more to her than a good friend. The awkwardness came as no surprise to her. She'd known it would be like this between them once he knew. That was why she'd fought so long and so hard to hide it from him.

She pulled her hand from his then, satisfied that it wasn't bleeding anymore, and shoved it into the pocket of her jacket.

Though it had stopped raining by mid-morning, the unseasonably cool weather still lingered. Shelly felt chilled to the bone.

"Come on," Brian said softly, closer than she'd believed him to be. "It's time to go."

"I think I'm going to stay for a while."

She heard the sound of car doors closing and engines starting in the distance. When she glanced around her, she saw no one but him, save for the men with their shovels standing off to the side. They'd come a little closer than they had been before, and she knew she didn't have much time left.

"Come on, Shel," Brian said, not waiting for an answer this time. He put an arm around her shoulders and propelled her toward the car, giving her no choice but to walk away with him. He opened the door for her, but she didn't get in. Not yet.

Shelly heard a strange motorized rumbling, and when she turned her head, she realized it was the sound of the coffin being lowered into the ground. The men were there with their shovels, ready to finish the job.

Shelly swallowed hard and waited for it to begin. This part had terrified her at her mother's funeral. She couldn't understand why they were putting her mother into the ground. After all, her father had taken such pains to explain to her that her mother was going to heaven.

Shelly had been sure that someone had made some dreadful mistake, and she'd tried to tell them, but she hadn't been able to make them understand. Despite all her tears and screams and pleas, she hadn't been able to convince them to stop.

She wondered if all of this was ever going to stop. Was she destined to be all alone on this earth? Some people were, she believed. Maybe she was one of them.

She flinched at that distinctive sound of dirt being thrown on top of a coffin.

"Shelly," Brian said, taking her by the arms and turning her gently to face him. "You don't need to see this. You know you don't."

She realized she was breathing hard, knew she was probably scaring him, and she tried to remember if she'd ever told him that awful story about her mother's funeral.

She must have, she decided. She'd told him everything when she'd been a child and he'd been her hero.

"It's time to go," he said. "It's cold out here, and you're shaking."

Yes. It took her a while to figure out that he was right; she was shaking. But she still wasn't ready to get into his car and leave this place.

Brian pulled her behind an old tree so that its massive trunk blocked her view of the grave, and he stood rigidly at her side. "You know," he said, once he had her full attention. "I'll always be here for you."

The breath left her body in a rush. She didn't like the way he'd read her emotions so easily and that he'd known exactly what she needed to hear.

"For as long as you'll let me," he vowed. "For as long as you want me. You still believe that, don't you, Shel?"

"Yes," she said, the word not much more than a sob. He'd said the same thing to her, maybe not the exact words, but the same sentiments, when she was ten or eleven years old.

She'd believed in him, too. She still did.

When her father had died, he'd been incredible. She didn't think she'd ever loved him or needed him more. She'd felt so alone, and he'd been an anchor for her. She'd clung to him then, on a day much like today, in another cemetery, six years ago.

"Oh, Brian."

"Just explain something to me," he said. "Try to explain it to yourself at the same time. Tell me why the hell you won't let me help you now?"

Why? Because she'd depended upon him forever. Because she'd wanted him forever. Because she was twenty-six years old and she couldn't keep waiting for him forever. Because right now she was more vulnerable than she'd ever been in her life.

She could easily give him a dozen reasons, if she could have gotten a word past her throat.

"I hate this," he said, his hands in a white-knuckle grip at his sides. "I can't stand it."

She jumped when he brought his fist down hard against the trunk of the tree.

"Isn't there something I can do? Anything? To fix this damned mess I've made of things?"

Wordlessly she shook her head back and forth and hugged her arms to her chest.

"I want to help you, Shel. I have to. I can't stand seeing you this way and not being able to do anything about it, and I hate the part I've played in making you this miserable."

"It's not your fault," she said, wondering if he was talking about one night or her whole life. She was thinking of both of them.

He couldn't help the way he felt. He couldn't help it that she wanted things from him she couldn't have. And he hadn't forced her into anything that night in Tallahassee.

She'd gone willingly, even eagerly, into his arms, and she'd known from the start that it would most likely lead to nothing but heartbreak. She'd dreamed about being with him for all of her adult life, and there was no way she could have turned down the chance to be with him that night.

"Well, if it's not my fault," he said, "then who the hell's fault is it?"

"Nobody's," she said.

"Then how did everything get so damned screwed up?"

"I don't know. I don't know much of anything anymore. I just... I miss Charlie. I miss my father and my mother and...."

She should have closed her eyes or turned away then. She should have done something to block the image of him standing there in front of her.

Rock solid, she'd told herself more than once, and the description had never been more fitting. He was a man a woman could depend upon, one whom she could trust with her life.

He would find someone to love some day, someone who'd love him back, and she would be one lucky woman. It wouldn't be Shelly, but that couldn't stop the longing inside her for him.

"I miss you," she told him.

"I miss you, too, Shelly." He held his arms open wide to her. "Let me help you now."

And she did. She simply didn't have the strength to resist so tempting an offer. She didn't even have to take that first step toward him. She opened her arms, and he filled them.

Nothing had ever felt so right as his arms hauling her up against him in a fierce embrace. She felt the need in him, maybe as strong as it was in her, just to feel her body against his.

She needed this desperately, needed this touch more than she needed her next breath. And as always, she didn't see how she was ever going to be able to let him go.

That afternoon after the reading of the will, Brian and Shelly found themselves in a meeting with Charlie Williams's attorney, George Ayers, about what would happen to the engineering firm and to Charlie's personal assets.

The will had been simple and exactly what Shelly had expected. Charlie had left everything to his wife, but the rest of it was hard to take in.

George Ayers didn't waste a lot of time mincing his words. He got right to the point. He was afraid Charlie was broke.

"How could he be broke?" Shelly asked.

"I'm not sure that he is now," the attorney said. "We'll have to gather up his financial records and see. But he was close to it the last time he spoke to me about it. And he was quite concerned about what would happen to his wife if, by chance, he happened to pass away before she did."

Brian jumped in. "What about the business? It had to be making money for him."

"Maybe it is now. I hope so. But there was a time several years ago, before his wife went into the nursing home, that the business was on the brink of bankruptcy. Apparently he'd been spending too much time away from it, and things had started to deteriorate."

"I know that was true in the past," Shelly said, "but I thought he'd turned things around."

"I hope he has, for his wife's sake. That's why I wanted to meet with the two of you today," the attorney said, pulling a thick file in front of him. "His wife's medical care is quite expensive. . . ."

"What about the insurance?" Brian asked.

"They have no health insurance. When his wife's medical bills started mounting, the insurance company raised the premiums so high, Mr. Williams couldn't pay them anymore. And no one would write a new policy that would cover her condition."

Shelly had known that, but still, she never thought Charlie was under the kind of financial pressure that came with a possible bankruptcy.

The attorney flipped through some papers and came up with the one he wanted. "Here it is," he said. "When he was here last, Mr. Williams was paying in excess of thirty-five thousand dollars a year for his wife's nursing-home care alone."

Brian whistled at the sum.

"So what's going to happen to her now?" Shelly asked.

"I'm not sure," the attorney said. "We'll have to see what kind of assets Charlie had left."

"Is there any life insurance?" Brian asked.

"There was a few years ago, but I'm not sure if he was able to keep paying the premiums. And even if he did, we have to wonder whether the money will be eaten up by his debts."

"What about the business?"

"Will it have to be sold?" Shelly hated that idea.

"If we can find someone who's willing to buy it," Ayers said. "I'm not sure what kind of value it would have. Many times the value of a small business is tied up in the owner's presence and his expertise in running it. Without that owner, we often see little value left in a business."

"What can we do?" Shelly asked.

"Well, Mrs. Williams is going to need every penny her husband has left. He was very concerned that she stay in the private nursing home where she is now until all his assets are exhausted. Unfortunately I don't think that's going to take long. But then that's where the two of you come in."

He turned to Brian. "He's asked that you run the business in his absence until it's either sold or closed. I understand that's something you've done before when he's been away."

"Yes," Brian said.

"I hope you're willing to do so again."

"Of course," he said.

"Good. Mr. Williams has directed us to place all his assets in trust for his wife, and he's asked that Miss Wilkerson oversee his wife's trust fund and serve as her legal guardian, since her medical condition has left her unable to oversee her own affairs.

"He's told me that he trusts you implicitly, Miss Wilkerson, and that he's sure you'll do the best you can to see that his wife is well cared for in whatever time she has left."

Then why didn't he tell me what was wrong? Shelly thought. Why didn't he trust me enough to let me help him? What had he been caught in the middle of, and why did this have to happen to him?

"This is a big responsibility," the lawyer said, looking at her. "There are a lot of decisions relating to her medical condition and treatment that you'll have to make, in addition to the financial decisions. I hope you're willing to assume those duties."

"Yes," she said, so overwhelmed by all that had happened in the past week she was practically numb to it all now.

Marion Williams. She closed her eyes and pictured the woman the last time she'd seen her, to tell her about Charlie's death. She'd thought Shelly was her daughter, and she'd acted as if she hadn't comprehended a word Shelly had said about Charlie.

And now it was up to Shelly to see that the woman was taken care of. It was an awesome responsibility, not unlike that of caring for a child. Marion was quite childlike in the advanced stages of her disease.

Shelly was still stunned by it all.

"What do we do first?" Brian asked, stepping in when she didn't seem to be able to do so.

"Most of all, we need to see where we are as far as the assets are concerned," the attorney said. "We'll need a complete inventory of his personal and professional assets. We could hire someone to do that, but it could be expensive and..."

"Why don't you let us see what we can get together for you before you hire someone to come in and do it," Brian said.

"Of course," Shelly agreed. "The business records should be no problem. Most everything's on Charlie's computer at the office."

He'd taken to keeping his own books in the past couple of years, ever since he'd computerized the accounting system. He liked to control every little aspect of the business. It took up a lot of his time, but that hadn't seemed to bother Charlie. Once he'd put his wife in the nursing home, he'd done nothing but work and visit with her.

"Well, now that we have that taken care of," the attorney said, reaching for another envelope. "I have a set of Mr. Williams's keys for his house, his car, his office and his safe-deposit box. I'll give those to you, along with a list he made a year ago of his assets."

Shelly took the keys and found herself staring at them while she listened to some of the more technical legal procedures they would go through before the will was probated and she was actually made Marion Williams's legal guardian.

The attorney finally stood and held out his hand to Brian, then to her, as she hastily rose from her chair and clutched the keys.

"I'll be waiting to hear from you both about what we have to work with for Mrs. Williams's trust fund," he said.

Chapter 12

It was strange to be at Charlie's house, searching the ring of keys she held in her hand to find the one that fit the front door. He'd never be here again. And now she and Brian were expected to sift through all his things, hoping to find something of value that would allow his wife to live the rest of her life in whatever comfort was to be found at that expensive nursing home where she was staying.

"Sure you want to do this?" Brian asked again as he stood beside her on the front steps.

They'd come there after meeting with the attorney.

"I don't think I'll be able to sleep at night, wondering about what's going to happen to poor Marion. What would they do to her if there's no money to pay her bills? Put her out into the street?"

"I don't know, Shel."

"I guess I need to call tomorrow and see when the next payment is due and to tell them... I don't even know. What am I going to tell them?"

"We'll work something out," he said. "Surely Charlie has some assets."

The last key she tried fit the door, and Shelly pushed it open, but hesitated about going inside. She felt as if she'd been to hell and back in the past week. The trip with Brian, the plane crash, the wedding night, Charlie's death.

She hadn't had time to get used to one disaster before the next one hit.

Brian's hand came up against her back, and she was too tired to try to escape from his touch right now.

"We don't have to do this tonight," he said.

"I know. I just want to gather up some of his papers to look over tonight at my apartment."

She knew she wouldn't sleep, no matter how hard she tried. And she didn't know how much time she had until the next payment was due to Marion's nursing home.

Shelly forced herself to walk across the threshold and search for the switch for the lights. They flooded the darkened house, illuminating a sparsely furnished living room, a hallway and a staircase.

"It's not much to look at, is it?" Brian said.

"No."

"I was hoping we'd at least be able to find some equity in his home, but this place..."

"He sold his home three years ago, and I'm sure that money's already gone. This house was just...a place to sleep, sometimes to eat a meal."

Brian walked through the living room to the age-worn rolltop desk that sat against the wall separating the living room from the kitchen. The top rolled up easily, revealing stacks of letters and papers in the wooden slots along the back of the desk's surface, but the two big file drawers on either of the legs wouldn't budge.

"Locked," he said. "Why don't you try the key set while I look around for a box to put some of this stuff in."

"Okay."

Shelly tried each of the six keys she'd been given, but none of them fit. She supposed she should search for another key, but now that she was here, she found herself reluctant to start rummaging through Charlie's personal things just yet.

She still remembered how difficult it had been to sort through all her father's possessions and close up his house. There were so many memories piled into the boxes and the drawers and the closets, so many emotions churned up by the process.

And now Charlie had asked her to do the same thing for him.

She wasn't sure she was up to it, but she couldn't walk away from it, either. She'd simply have to find a way to do it. He was counting on her, and this was one of the last things she'd ever do for him.

Grimly, she resigned herself to the task ahead of her. She opened the middle desk drawer, just to prove to herself that she could do it. She found papers, paper clips, rubber bands, postage stamps, ink pens, a stapler, everything but keys.

Shelly shoved the drawer back into place and shivered, wondering if it was really that cold in the house or if she was simply chilled from the inside out.

"Found a box," Brian said. "Did you get the drawers open?"

"No. Maybe the keys are at the office."

He started piling the papers from the wooden slots into the cardboard box, pinning together the ones from the same slots with paper clips.

"That's odd," he said, looking down at the locked drawers. "He lives alone. Why would he lock up his own papers in his own house?"

"I don't know . . . habit, maybe?"

Brian's look said he doubted that.

"He was a good man, Brian."

"I know, but sometimes good people get caught up in very bad things."

They emptied the desk of the papers they had access to and decided to worry about the rest of them later. Shelly had more than enough to keep her busy for the evening, so they headed back to her apartment. Brian carried the box in and set it on the table.

"How about a cup of coffee?" he said as he took off his raincoat and loosened his tie.

And Shelly knew then that it was going to be a battle to get rid of him tonight.

"I'm really tired, Brian." She didn't sit down. She didn't invite him in. She just waited there by the door, hoping he would take the hint and go. Of course, he didn't. He could be incredibly obtuse when it suited him.

"Then you sit down," he said, coming to help her slip out of her coat. "I'll make the coffee."

She knew the man was deliberately misunderstanding her, but it was going to take a while before she had the strength to challenge him on it.

And as she sat there, tired to the bone and mentally exhausted, she realized for the first time what Charlie Williams had done to her. He'd tied her life together with Brian Sandelle's for months to come. She'd be working more closely with him than she ever had as they both tried to salvage something from Charlie's estate to help his poor, sick wife.

She'd counted on getting away from him within a matter of weeks. She'd answered a few announcements of job vacancies in a couple of the trade journals on Tuesday, and if she hadn't heard from someone soon, she was going to consider resigning, anyway, going somewhere and living for as long as she could on her meager savings. She was that desperate.

And now she couldn't do that. She had an obligation to Charlie and to his wife, one that would tie her to the area for an indefinite period of time.

"Oh, God," she said loud enough for Brian to hear.

He walked into the living room as she stood from the sofa, and her distress must have been evident on her face. He was watching her intently.

"I'm really tired, Brian, and I think it's time you went home."

He shook his head back and forth. "I don't think you should be alone tonight."

"I'm alone every night," she said, hoping she didn't sound bitter about that.

"But you don't bury a good friend every night."

No, thankfully, she didn't.

"I'll be fine," she insisted. "I'm used to being here by myself."

"Well, you don't have to be, not tonight."

He put his hand on her arm, touching her easily, testing her reaction. She forced herself to move slowly as she pulled away from him. She heard him curse with a barely veiled anger in his voice, and she flinched at the sound.

"I know," he said, trying to make amends, "I'm not supposed to do that. I'm supposed to just stand back and watch while you're hurting like hell and I do nothing." He was still angry. He couldn't hide it. Soon he gave up trying.

"So sue me," he said. "I happen to have this undeniable urge to take care of you. I always have, and it's so damned hard to turn it off, especially now that you're hurting so badly and I'm part of the reason."

Shelly didn't know what to say. She didn't have the strength. She didn't have the will.

"Could I just hold you?" he said. "Just for a minute."

She shook her head.

"It helped," he said. "Didn't it? Just a little, back at the cemetery?"

A little, she admitted, but only to herself. It had helped, and it had hurt, both at the same time.

But as much as she wanted to lean on him right now, she couldn't. She'd leaned on him her whole life, and she simply couldn't do that at the same time she was determined to put him out of her life and out of her dreams.

"I don't want to cry anymore, Brian. I don't want to lean on anyone, and I don't want anyone to hold me," she said, although she was incredibly ambivalent about the holding. "I just want to be left alone."

"Shelly—"

"Listen to me," she insisted. "I'm not your responsibility. I never have been. I don't want you hovering over me or worrying about me or taking care of me or feeling sorry for me. God, don't do that. Don't do any of it. It's not your job."

"I never saw it as a job or a responsibility. It's just…the way things have always been."

"No," she said, more strongly than she realized she was capable of at that moment. "It's the way things were a long time ago between us. But not anymore.

"It's been years, Brian. Years. Things have changed. I've changed."

"I know," he said.

"Then please don't make this any harder for me than it already is."

"Shelly, I care about you a great deal. You do know that, at least, don't you?"

"Yes," she admitted.

"I'm just trying to make things easier for you, but you won't let me."

"Maybe I can't. Did you ever think of that? Did you ever think that it's hard just to be with you? Just to be in the same room with you?"

"Why?" he said flatly.

She had nothing else to lose, so she simply told him. "You can't give me what I need."

"How do you know? You've never told me what you need from me."

She would have laughed, if it hadn't sounded so ridiculous. As if all she had to do was ask for what she wanted from him....

"I just need to be left alone," she said, truly wanting just that from him.

"No, you don't. That's the last thing you need tonight."

And, obviously, the last thing she was going to get from him. What in the world was she going to do? Shelly wondered. She was so tired of fighting herself and him both, so tired of trying desperately to hide all her feelings from him.

"Come on, Shel." He was quietly serious now, his eyes intent on her and his mouth set in a firm, thin line. "We've been dancing around this for days. We can't dance forever."

God help her, she'd seen it coming from the time of that awful morning-after scene at the hotel, and she simply hadn't known how to stop it. "I just...I don't see the point in going into this."

"I do. We made love that night."

She shook her head, coming closer to hating him than she ever had in her life. Why did he have to know? Why did it mean so much to him, anyway? Was his conscience bothering him? She'd gladly forgive him for what he'd done, if only he'd let it remain her secret and not theirs to share.

"Did you really think you could hide it from me forever?" he asked.

Shelly didn't say a word. This was so humiliating, probably more so than the night it had happened. Because his memory of tonight would be crystal clear, and it would always be between them.

"Did you really think that once my head cleared I wouldn't realize the differences between you and her?"

Shelly felt absolutely ill, just as she had during that long night. She'd sat curled up in a chair in the living room of the suite all night, trying to figure out what to do next, while he slept like the dead in the other room.

It had been the worst night of her life—until now.

"Don't do this to me, Brian."

"I know it happened," he said. "Your scent was still clinging to my skin the next morning."

Just as his had clung to her. She'd been trembling badly as she scrubbed it off.

"I may not remember the whole night in my mind, but my body remembers," he said. "It remembers just how your body felt beneath mine. It remembers—"

"Keep it up." She dared him with all the bitterness in her soul. "And you might just make me hate you."

"We made love that night," he insisted.

"You made love to Rebecca that night."

And with that admission she was deadly calm, her mind cleared in an instant of everything else but what she had just done.

Shelly closed her eyes and wondered if it was too late to catch the last plane out of Naples tonight. And she wondered if, once again, he'd come running after her, with his guilty conscience driving him on.

She didn't want his guilt. She didn't want his pity. She wanted the passion he'd shown her that night. It was the stuff that haunted her dreams. Except, of course, in her dreams his passion was for her and her alone.

"Damn you, Brian Sandelle!" she said, wishing she could forget all he had shown her that night.

She should never have allowed it to happen. She could have stopped it. He hadn't forced her. But she hadn't been able to bring herself to stop him. She'd known that it was the only chance she'd ever get to be with him. She'd known, too, that she'd regret it.

What woman could come face-to-face with her fantasy man and turn him away?

Certainly not her.

Well, she thought, she'd gone and done it now. Too late to retreat. Maybe it always had been. She didn't see now how she could have hoped to hide it from him for long, anyway, and it made her furious.

She went with the anger, letting it bubble up inside her. "There," she told him. "You got it out of me. Are you satisfied now?"

Perversely, she took some pleasure in seeing that she'd been the one to hurt him now.

But the pleasure didn't last. Nerves overrode it.

He looked . . . dangerous, she decided. Like a lion who's sighted his prey, he started closing in on her. He came closer and closer. She stood rooted to the spot, knowing she should run, yet knowing it wouldn't do any good.

Just when she was sure he wouldn't stop until he had his body flush against hers, her back truly against the wall, he did.

He was still leaning over her, his eyes blazing down into hers, her back actually pressing against the wall in a vain effort to get away.

"Satisfied?" He spit out the word in disgust, with him or with her, she couldn't say. "Not by a long shot."

And, in a move for which she'd be eternally grateful, he reached around her right side, opened the front door and left.

Brian could have kicked himself right then and there, especially for that last line, but the whole situation was so damned frustrating. He sat in the car outside Shelly's apartment, watching the lights go off one by one, wondering if she was sitting alone in the dark and crying because of him, again.

How could this have happened to them? He was a careful and cautious man. He was raised to treat a woman with the utmost respect, and he'd always done that.

He'd never hurt a woman the way he'd managed to hurt Shelly. And the awful irony was that he cared for her more deeply than any woman in his life, save for his mother and the woman he'd once planned to make his wife.

And what had he done? Selfishly he'd pulled her into the middle of one of the worst days in his life—Rebecca's wedding day. He'd screwed up his own head royally with a stupid combination of prescription drugs and alcohol, and then he'd made love to her.

And called her Rebecca.

Brian swore harshly, regrets and recriminations making a bitter mixture inside him.

How was he going to make this up to her? How could he make things right between them? He just didn't see what he could do to make it right.

Although, if he could get his head screwed on straight, he was sure he could find a way to do it.

Trouble was, he simply couldn't think straight anymore. He was too busy trying to recall every minute detail of what it had felt like to have her naked and warm and willing beneath him in the bed that night.

"Damn," he said aloud in the darkened car. Those kind of thoughts hadn't gotten him anywhere.

How could he think of her that way? This was Shelly, the scrawny little kid with the puppy-dog eyes and mangled braids that her father never quite figured out how to make. He kept thinking of her that way. At least, he tried. He couldn't handle the reality of the woman.

What a damned mess he'd made of things.

His judgment was obviously shot all to hell these days. The woman he'd loved forever, the one he'd believe he'd spend the rest of his life with, had dumped him for another man. He still had trouble believing that. It wasn't that his ego was so big he couldn't imagine losing a woman to another man. It was the years he'd spent when he'd been absolutely certain that he and Rebecca were meant to be together.

Obviously they hadn't.

And now? Now the woman he'd thought of with sisterly affection and devotion for going on twenty years—he'd taken her to bed with him. Brian could only think of one reason why she would have gone, a reason that only made things worse. Obviously she cared for him, and not in the innocent way he cared for her.

Brian wondered how long she'd felt that way, wondered how many times in the past he'd hurt her without even realizing it.

And then he'd taken her to bed with him. It was absolutely unforgivable, he knew. So was wanting to make love to her again.

Chapter 13

Brian didn't get much sleep that night, but the dreams he had were worth losing sleep over. Shelly was driving him insane, and he was handling the whole situation badly. He pushed her when he should have backed away, time and time again.

The work-related problems weren't helping, either, and he was worried about Shelly being caught in the middle of it. He was afraid they might be in real danger, that Charlie hadn't had any accident, that he'd been murdered and the tampering with the plane had simply been the first attempt to get rid of the man.

He wanted Shelly out of here, but he didn't see how he'd be able to talk her into leaving. And he wanted things cleared up quickly. He needed to be free to concentrate on her and her alone.

He didn't know what this thing between them was. He didn't know when it had all begun or where it would lead them, but he intended to find out. Until then, he wouldn't let the woman out of his sight for long.

So that's why, at a little before seven the next morning, he was standing outside her apartment with two cups of steaming coffee and a bag of what might as well have been pure sugar.

Shelly had a weakness for sugar—at least, she used to.

He was counting on that alone to get him inside the door to her apartment this morning. He wondered if she did hate him, if not for the things he had done, then for the way he'd left her no choice but to tell him about what had happened between them that night.

And he kept remembering when he'd asked her before if he'd hurt her that night. "Not that way," she'd told him. Not her body, but her feelings—not that one was any easier to excuse than the other.

No, he thought, resigned to it now. She wasn't going to be happy to see him. He'd expected that when he rang the bell. He'd come prepared for that, with a bag full of bribery from the bakery on the corner.

He hadn't been prepared to find her hair still wet from the shower, her cheeks still pink from the steam, or her body encased in what he'd bet was that damned man's shirt and nothing else.

"What do you want?" she demanded, peering through the narrow opening—all that was allowed by the chain lock that was still in place.

He swallowed hard and held up the foam cup for her to see. "I brought coffee."

"I have my own coffee."

He turned to his secret weapon, still warm from the oven, and hoped the smell alone would keep her mind off what he had put her through the night before.

"I brought breakfast." He held the bag practically under her nose.

She stood there for a minute. Brian couldn't help himself. Through the narrow opening in the doorway, he watched while a drop of water fell from the end of one of her curls to the open V-neck of the shirt, then trailed downward to her...

Damn. This wasn't the way he'd planned to start this day.

When he wasn't looking, she reached through the door for the bag.

"Wait a minute," he said, snatching it away just in time. "I was counting on these to get me inside at least." He'd known he'd never have made it in on his own.

"A bag of doughnuts?" she said indignantly. As she tilted her head to the side, another drop of water fell from the ends of her hair.

"Chocolate doughnuts," he said, his throat tighter than he would have liked. "With chocolate icing."

She liked chocolate, hopefully more than she disliked him at the moment.

Her mouth opened, then snapped closed again. She looked from the bag to him, then back to the bag again.

"We can eat them while they're still warm if you hurry up and make up your mind," he said.

It was close, but the smell must have done it. She unchained the door, then held it open while he came inside.

Brian knew better than to waste any time handing over the goods. Shelly took the coffee, watching him the whole time while she peeled off the lid and had her first sip.

Business, he told himself, watching her mouth curl around the rim of the cup. He'd planned to keep things strictly business this morning.

They would dispose of the business problems, then get on with the personal side of things. It was a good plan, a logical plan, one that would have seen him through this mess.

But he'd forgotten certain things, and he was discovering some new things, as well—like how good she looked, still dripping from the shower. And that damned shirt—he hadn't expected to get jealous all over again, wondering about the man who'd once worn that shirt or the situation in which he'd come to give it to her.

It wasn't doing his head a damned bit of good to wonder about what the man still meant to her or why she still wore his shirt. Neither had he realized, when he'd headed for the bakery, how sexy a woman savoring a chocolate-covered doughnut could be.

Brian set his coffee down on the counter before he spilled it.

Below the ends of that long shirt were a pair of smooth, sleek thighs that were, from what he remembered, surprisingly strong. He wondered if she still liked to ride her bike and whether she wore those skintight workout pants that cyclists favored.

Her hair was still dripping, and the front of the shirt was getting damp, clinging to her skin in a way that made the curves of her breasts all the more obvious. And she'd gotten a little of the chocolate icing caught at the corner of her mouth. He wanted to fix that, and he had a feeling, from the way she'd flushed all over again, that she knew it, too.

"Why are you here?" she asked, catching him staring at her.

She had to know what this thing she was wearing was doing to him, and she'd made no move to go put on a robe or something else—anything else.

Was she testing him? Or tormenting him? Hell, what did it matter, anyway. Whatever she was doing, it was working.

"We've got some work to do," he said, desperately trying to stick to the plan he'd made, despite the temptation to do otherwise.

He watched the fingertips of her left hand search in vain for the chocolate smear on her lips, and he wanted to find it for her. He wanted that very much.

So much for a clear head. Brian worked to clear his throat instead and tried to ignore her mouth. "The financial records," he managed to say. "It's Saturday. The office is deserted. I thought we could spend the day sorting through things there."

She nodded warily.

"We are going to have to work together to get to the bottom of this," he said.

"I know. I just..."

Hoped that she would find a way out of doing that with him?

Yes, he knew she'd be wondering just that. That was why he'd felt it was important to get here first thing in the morning, to catch her before she'd had a chance to rebuild her defenses against him.

"I'm going to the office," he said, trying not to sound as if he cared whether or not she joined him. "I can go by myself or..."

"I'll go with you. Give me a minute to get dressed."

Gladly, he thought, not allowing himself to turn around and watch her walk out of the room. He gulped at his own hot coffee then, not caring that it was burning his mouth as it went down.

A damned doughnut, he thought. That and some jerk's dress shirt was all it took to leave him here with his brain short-circuited all over again, in a matter of seconds.

* * *

She was dressed in minutes. Brian was amazed. He hadn't known it was possible for a woman to get ready that quickly.

She'd put on jeans. How long had it been since he'd seen her in a pair of jeans? They weren't that tight. They just clung to every curve. She had some very nice curves, and he wasn't sure when that had happened. She'd been such a scrawny little kid, all arms and legs and pigtails.

Well, as she'd been trying to tell him, she wasn't a kid anymore.

She had on a plain red T-shirt, tucked into the jeans. There shouldn't have been anything sexy at all about that, but there was.

She'd braided her still-wet hair. She didn't have any makeup on, just lots of smooth, soft skin. She did have this incredible peaches-and-cream complexion, and she blushed so easily. Her eyes were a warm brown, her mouth wide and generous.

She must not have even looked in a mirror, because that speck of chocolate was still there, caught in the corner of her lips.

Damn.

"Something wrong?" she asked.

No, he told himself. Don't do it. Don't you dare touch her. But he did. Inside of five minutes and he'd already abandoned his carefully thought-out plan. All for an enticing speck of chocolate on those warm, soft lips of hers.

"You have ... a little bit of chocolate—" he put up his hand to brush it away "—right here."

Her lips parted as his fingers cupped her jaw and his thumb settled into the corner of her mouth, and if he'd had any sense left at all, he would have stopped at that.

Instead, he left his hand there, against her soft cheek. "Wait a minute," he said when she would have pulled away.

He moved slowly, giving her time to get away, if she wanted to do that. But she never tried. He fit his lips to the corner of hers and brushed them lightly with his tongue. "I didn't get it all."

She didn't move. He doubted she was even breathing. God knows, he wasn't.

She smelled of some perfumed soap from the shower and tasted of chocolate and cream. He caught just a hint of it as his tongue teased her upper lips, working its way slowly from one end of them to the other, not daring to slip in between them, into her mouth.

Her lips parted easily, her breath mingling with his, as he found a bit of the sweet, sticky mixture and licked it off her lips.

His body roared to life, his arousal straining against the confines of his jeans, and he knew he couldn't let himself pull her any closer to him.

"Damn," he muttered, the frustration eating at him. He grabbed for her too harshly when she finally tried to move away from him. "Wait a minute, please," he said, easing his hold, then dropping his hands from her arms altogether.

He'd frightened her, and that was the last thing he wanted to do.

"I don't understand any of this," he said, knowing it explained nothing, that it excused nothing in his behavior, but not knowing what else he could tell her at that moment.

Besides, it was the truth. He didn't understand any of this.

"It's not that hard to understand," she said. "Rebecca's gone, and I'm here. I'm...available. At least, you think I am."

"That's not it at all." He was sure of that. "Do you think I haven't tried to find someone to take her place? You remember the years she spent with Tucker, the times I didn't think I had a chance with her, even once she'd divorced him. And it's been almost a year since she broke our engagement. Believe me, I tried to forget about her with a half-dozen women, and it's never worked.''

Instead, it left a bitter taste in his mouth and an even emptier feeling inside him. It had always been better simply to be alone.

Until now.

"I won't be your substitute for her," she said, standing her ground.

"I'm not looking for one." And he wasn't. He hadn't realized it until just this moment, but he felt curiously free of Rebecca Malloy. It was a strange feeling, one that would take a while to get used to. Ever since he'd been a boy, Rebecca had been there.

While the other teenagers were looking at a picture in a magazine, Brian was looking at the girl next door. Rebecca had colored his perception of all the other women he met for so long. He hadn't thought he'd ever escape that.

But he had.

Because of the woman standing in front of him? The woman she'd become when he hadn't been paying any attention? He couldn't say. And he had no right to touch her like that, kiss her like that, until he knew.

He'd hurt her enough already.

Brian shook his head, but it didn't help to clear it at all. He threw up his hands at his sides. "I don't understand any of this."

"Let me know when you do," she said, looking so fragile, so breakable, it frightened him.

He could so easily hurt her again. He wondered how much he'd hurt her already—before the wedding night—when he hadn't even realized she had feelings for him.

And he wondered exactly what sort of feelings they were.

Did she love him? Did she think she did? She said she'd been with that other man, hoping he could help her forget someone else.

He groaned at the thought—her with another man, all the while wishing that man was someone else. Brian knew how rotten that felt. He'd done it before, and he hated the idea of her going through that, as well.

So what was this thing between them? He was afraid to even put a name on it. It was still so new to him, so overwhelming and all-powerful.

"Are we going to work this morning?" she asked finally from the spot across the room where she'd retreated.

"Sure," he said. "Let's go."

Work, he told himself as he drove them to the office. Concentrate on that and that alone. He didn't have a prayer otherwise.

He was anxious to start digging into Charlie Williams's files, anyway. He wanted to know what the man had been up to, and he wanted to make sure that Shelly and the other people who worked for him weren't in any danger.

"This thing just gets more and more strange with every day that goes by," he said, pulling into the parking lot.

"Have you heard anything from the FAA yet about the plane?" she asked.

"No, and I doubt we'll hear anything more soon. It may well be a year or more before they give us an answer for sure."

"What about the sheriff? Is he at least investigating Charlie's death as a murder?"

"Not yet. He did send the body to Miami for an autopsy, but it came back inconclusive." He slid into a parking space, glad to see that the lot was empty save for his car.

"How did he die?"

Brian would have taken her hand then in an instinctive gesture of comfort, but…things had changed between them. He had to get used to that. "He drowned," he said simply.

"In four or five feet of water?"

Brian shrugged. "Remember, it was raining that day they found him and the day before. The river's a main drainage route for part of the county. Apparently the water levels fluctuate quite a bit, depending on the weather.

"But there was something else," he said. "There was some blow to his head, but no one could tell whether he hit his head in the fall or whether someone hit him and then dumped his body in the river.

"I'm sorry," he said. "I know he meant a great deal to you." Brian got out and went around the side of the car to open her door for her. They walked into the small office building the engineering firm shared with an accounting firm and an architectural firm.

"Did you find anything in the records from Charlie's house?" he asked as they made their way up the stairs.

"It was mostly medical bills. Thousands of dollars in bills, all of them paid. I guess we know where his money went."

"There has to be a connection to all of this," he said.

He ran through the firm's client list in his mind. They had a lot of big-time clients.

Charlie Williams was born and raised in Tallahassee, the state capital. That's where he and Brian's father had become friends.

Charlie did a lot of contract work for the state years ago, and he still knew all the guys running the state highway department. Contractors who were looking to do business with the state often came to Charlie because of his connections. There wasn't anything that was necessarily dirty about that relationship. It was simply the way things were done.

People in charge knew Charlie. They respected him, and they trusted him. Every little edge a construction company could get could help. In fact, some of the biggest road and bridge contractors in the southern tip of the state did business with Charlie, most often using him for the state-required inspections of their work.

Brian's immediate suspicions concerned the company whose bridge work Charlie was inspecting at the time of his death. He hadn't had a chance to check in the past forty-eight hours. Things had been too crazy.

But he'd check today.

He was looking down at the keys in his hand, trying to come up with the correct one, so he was right upon the front door to the engineering office when he realized that Shelly wasn't with him any longer.

"What?" He turned to find her standing in the middle of the hall, two feet behind him.

"Look." She pointed to the engineering office's front door. It was standing halfway open.

At eight o'clock on a Saturday morning?

He held up a hand, motioning for her to stop outside the doorway, then listened.

No sound came from inside.

"Stay here," he whispered.

Cautiously he stepped into the entranceway and looked around.

"Damn," he muttered. The place was trashed. There were papers everywhere. Desks had been swept clean, the debris left littering the floor. Filing cabinets were overturned, the papers spewing out in all directions.

Brian walked through the paper trail to Charlie's office and, just as he suspected, the destruction was even worse here.

"Brian?" Shelly called out.

He took one more look around, satisfied that they had the place to themselves. "Come on back," he said. "I'm in Charlie's office, and whoever did this is long gone."

Nothing was left in place. It would take days to sort out this mess, days to even figure out what was gone. Although he spotted one thing right away—the diskette case by Charlie's computer was empty.

Brian turned on the machine and searched through its memory. Just as he suspected—blank. Everything had been erased.

He wondered how many of the other computers in the office had been cleared of their information, as well.

Still, at the moment, this little computer of Charlie's was the worst blow. Every bit of the firm's financial records was in that computer.

"Tell me there's a hard copy or a copy on disk of the financial records," he said to Shelly.

"There has to be," she said. "If we can ever find them in this mess."

"Exactly," he said, picking up the phone to call the police. "Think about this with me. What don't they want us to find? And who doesn't want us to find it? What could be in this office that someone would kill for?"

They were tied up all morning with the city police department trying to figure out what—if anything—had been taken. So far they hadn't found anything missing.

Then they spent the afternoon trying to put the place back together again. Brian called in the secretaries and the receptionist, who did double duty as a billing clerk. He found out that she had access to surprisingly little of the firm's financial records, and that struck him as very odd.

He knew Charlie still thought of the firm as a small operation and that he liked to keep his hand in all aspects of the business. He also knew it didn't take that long to keep the books by computer, once you figured out the basic program.

But, as Brian saw it, there were a half-dozen more productive things Charlie could have been doing with his time. He certainly wouldn't fool with the finances now that he was in charge of the firm temporarily. He'd watch them closely, because the firm was in trouble, but he'd leave the bulk of it to the billing clerk or an accountant.

Shelly was with one of the secretaries now, combing through debris on the floor, trying to find some of the records.

He motioned for her to join him in the corner, out of earshot of the dozen people working in the office. "Got anything?" he asked.

"Very little," she said.

Brian shook his head. "There's no reason for Charlie to be keeping the books himself—unless he had something to hide."

"Maybe he just didn't want anyone to know how close he was to bankruptcy," Shelly said. "Maybe it was nothing more than his pride."

"Maybe," he said, but doubted it. "Have you gotten any more of those phone calls?"

"No," she said.

"You're sure you recognized the guy's voice."

"Yes. Is the sheriff looking for him?"

"He's a little more interested than he was before this happened at the office, but he hasn't made a lot of progress in finding the guy."

Brian didn't add that he'd love to find the guy himself. He wanted to know how he could have left Shelly here, knowing she was in danger. And he wanted to know if she had any feelings left for the guy now.

Business, he reminded himself. Stick to business—for now.

"Did Charlie and this guy work on any big projects together? Anything that you can remember?"

"I don't know," she said. "I don't remember."

"The client files are a mess, but it looks like most of them are still here, at least. We've got a chance of finding something there, if we knew what the hell we were looking for."

Chapter 14

Shelly was exhausted. They'd spent the entire day cooped up in that office, sorting through papers until the words and the numbers were swimming on the pages.

She was nearly asleep when the cessation of the car's movement roused her. She yawned and waited a moment for her eyes to adjust to the darkness.

Something wasn't right. The building in front of her was as big as her apartment building, but it wasn't her apartment.

"Where are we?" she asked, as the car slid into a garage.

"My house," Brian said.

"Oh." It was a breathless sound, much too meek and mild for her tastes. She tried again. "Why are we at your house?"

Brian opened his door so the interior light of the car clicked on, then scowled at the console as it broadcast an annoying beep. He went to pull the keys from the ignition to stop the noise, but they weren't cooperating, something that obviously annoyed him even more. He finally closed the door and clicked on the overhead light.

Shelly found it all quite fascinating. If she didn't know better, she would have said the man was flustered. But that couldn't be right. Brian Sandelle didn't get flustered.

"Don't fight me on this, Shel," he said.

"On what?"

"I'm not taking you back to your apartment tonight, not unless I go back there with you." He shifted in the seat, turning his upper body to face her. "This thing has gotten way out of hand. Charlie's dead, and whoever was after him has already missed once and nearly gotten both of us killed in the process."

She didn't say anything to that. She'd tried not to imagine the implications of the break-in at the office.

"The man's getting more dangerous by the minute," Brian said. "He's not even trying to hide things anymore. He trashed the office. Think about that."

"About what?" she said.

"He's brought everything out into the open now. He didn't have to trash the place. He could have just searched it, and it's likely no one would have been the wiser. But he left no doubt that he'd been there."

Shelly supposed that was true, but she still wanted to go back to her apartment.

"Look," Brian said. "We already knew the man was dangerous. Now he's getting desperate."

She hadn't thought of that. With the plane, with Charlie's so-called accident, there'd been nothing concrete that would prove anything had actually been tampered with—at least, nothing yet. But with his search of the office, there was no doubt. Something was going on. Someone wanted something from that office, and he obviously intended to get it.

"Okay," she said. "But what does it have to do with where I sleep."

"The man who searched the office knows where you sleep at night, for one thing. He went through the personnel records, too. If he didn't know where you lived before, he knows now."

"Well then, he knows where you live, too."

"And he'll have to get through me and my alarm system to get to you tonight."

Oh, no, Shelly thought. She wasn't spending another night with him. The two they'd already spent together had been more than enough.

"I think I'd really feel a lot better if I was at my own place."

"We can do it that way, but your place is a lot smaller than mine. You'll be tripping all over me, and I've seen that little thing you call a couch. I'm not crazy about the idea of trying to sleep on it."

And she wasn't crazy about the idea of tripping all over him in her little one-bedroom apartment, either. But she wanted so much to be alone.

"I don't think this is such a good idea, Brian."

"Got a better one? Because I'm not leaving you alone tonight."

She could go to a hotel, but she doubted that would satisfy him, either. And she certainly wasn't going to a hotel with him.

"Look," he said. "The man who used to live here had quite an art collection and an expensive security system to protect it. If anyone tries to get to you here, we'll know it long before he ever gets into the house. Besides, this place is huge. It has five bedrooms and seven bathrooms. You can take your pick."

She thought again about that hazy impression she'd gotten of the imposing stone structure. Shelly wondered if this was the house he'd planned to share with Rebecca. If it was, she didn't want to be anywhere near the place.

"Don't fight me on this, Shel. I'm worried about you, and you know I have reason to be worried."

"I'm a grown woman," she countered.

"I know."

"It's not—"

"Not my responsibility to watch out for you? Not my right? I'll grant you that. Maybe I'm being overly cautious—I'll give you that one, too. But could you just put up with it for a few days, for my sake? At least until we figure out what happened to Charlie and what that guy was looking for at the office today?"

A few days? She shuddered at the thought of spending her days and her nights with him until this thing was resolved.

"Okay, just for tonight?" he said, backing away. "And I promise, we can argue about it all you want tomorrow."

Still, she didn't say anything. She didn't know what to say. She was frightened of what was happening, and it seemed she hadn't slept soundly in days.

"You still trust me?" he said.

"Yes." There was no doubt about that.

"Shel, I'm beat. Let's go inside and go to sleep."

They went in through the garage door, which opened into a big laundry-storage room that was as big as her bedroom. He explained the security system to her and gave her the code to turn it on and off, then led the way into the kitchen.

It was huge, with heavy, rich mahogany cabinets, gleaming white tile countertops and matching tile flooring. Polished copper pots hung from a rack, suspended from the ceiling, but other than that and an empty glass in the sink,

Shelly saw no signs that anyone ever cooked a meal here. The place looked as if it had never been touched.

There were bar stools tucked under the counter, but no table or chairs in the eat-in kitchen area. Nothing in the formal dining room, either. She caught a glimpse of a huge fireplace in the living room, empty, as well.

He headed straight for the stairs, and she followed him.

"Did you just move in?" she said, trying to remember how long ago he'd told her about the house. Had he actually bought it? Or did he lease it with an option to buy? She couldn't remember.

"A few months ago," he hedged.

Six at least, she thought, remembering it had still been well before Thanksgiving. She knew for sure then. This was supposed to be Rebecca's house.

And already Shelly regretted giving in so easily when he'd insisted that she stay the night.

She could see Rebecca in this huge, elegant house. She'd know just what to do with it to make it as much of a showplace as her own childhood home or Brian's had been.

Shelly wouldn't know where to start to make something like that of this big, lonely house.

"There's a half bed set up in here, if this is all right," Brian said, pushing open the door and turning on the light. "It has its own bathroom, and my room's just across the hall."

And then she knew he'd probably put this little bed together for Sammy to sleep in the first time he and Rebecca came to visit, probably left the rest of the place empty so Rebecca could start from scratch in decorating it.

Yet here it stood, a beautiful, empty shell, a reminder of all that he must have wanted and all that he had lost.

Shelly wondered what it must be like for him, living in a big, empty house without the woman he loved.

* * *

She took what was supposed to be Sammy's bedroom, even if it was across the hall from Brian's.

He got her towels for the bathroom, some soap, shampoo, toothpaste and a toothbrush.

She was doing fine, she told herself, her face scrubbed clean, her teeth brushed, her hair loose from the braid. Then, when she came out of the bathroom, wondering what she was going to wear to sleep in, she saw a white dress shirt thrown across the half bed.

Shelly looked carefully around the room to make sure it was empty, then went to the door and locked it. She picked up the shirt, noting the way the ends fell to her knees and the sleeves nearly that far.

Brian's shirt, she thought, straight from the dry cleaners, she'd guessed by the starchy feel of it. At least it smelled of fabric softener and not like a man.

Reluctantly she stripped off her clothes and slid into the shirt, willing herself not to think of the man who wore it, the man who was sleeping across the hall from her. Strange that he would give her this to sleep in, she thought, lying down in the unfamiliar bed.

If she hadn't known better, she would have sworn he was jealous of Grant Edwards and the shirt the man had left behind.

Brian was jealous as hell of Grant Edwards and that damned shirt.

There was no way he was going to take her back to her apartment so she could get some of her things together, only to have her bring that shirt to his house to sleep in.

If she could sleep in his house, she could sleep in his shirt, as well.

He'd taken great pleasure in throwing one of his own on the bed for her, a clean, crisp white one that he thought would do wonders for her complexion and dark eyes.

And now, he suspected, he would spend the night wondering what she looked like in it.

Shelly slept for twelve straight hours and woke up starving. She slipped on the jeans she'd worn yesterday and tucked Brian's shirt into them, then made her way downstairs.

She wasn't at all surprised to find that there was next to nothing in the house to eat. At least there was coffee. While it brewed, she searched the front lawn for the Sunday paper, but found none. The man was positively uncivilized.

Obviously he didn't spend much time here, and Shelly could understand why he didn't.

The house made her sad. It would have to be so much worse for him.

Shelly forgot sometimes that all those emotions she'd experienced over the years, when she'd been sure Brian was the one she loved and that she'd never have him, he'd experienced, as well.

He knew every disappointment she did. What a thing for the two of them to share.

She wandered through his empty house, in his shirt and her jeans, waiting for him to wake up, wondering what the day would bring.

It was hard to believe that only a week had passed since they'd gone to Tallahassee for Rebecca's wedding. It seemed like a lifetime. If anyone had told her that her life could change so drastically in so little time, she wouldn't have believed them.

She wondered if Brian felt the same way. She wondered how much had changed for him.

She was more frightened than she'd ever been in her life over what she'd seen at the office yesterday. Charlie's death had left her as sad as she'd been since she lost her father. And Brian had her more confused than she'd ever been in her life.

She'd given up, dammit. It was long past time for her to give up on him, once and for all.

But now...

She couldn't hope. She couldn't let herself. She'd done it so many times before.

True, things had changed between them. She felt it in the way he watched her. But everything was so crazy now. If Brian was like she was, he'd hardly had time to think anything through. He couldn't know what he was feeling right now.

He was interested in her. She'd have to be the most naive woman in the world not to recognize that.

But a man's interest was such a fleeting thing. And he was bound to be a little interested now; after all, they'd slept together, and he had little, if any, memory of the event. He felt guilty about it, and he still had very strong protective instincts where she was concerned. That was all a part of it.

But what else was it? What else did he feel for her? It was much too soon to tell.

All she knew for sure was that she had to be very careful here. She was incredibly vulnerable where he was concerned. It would be so easy for her to get hurt all over again.

Once he'd finally fallen asleep Brian slept like the dead. He couldn't believe he'd been so out of it. He wandered into his bathroom, splashed some cold water on his face and brushed his teeth. It took him a minute to figure out why he'd put on a pair of pajama pants to sleep in when he usually wore nothing at all to bed.

And then he remembered Shelly was at his house.

He ran a hand through his unruly hair as he made his way through the bedroom and across the hall. "Shel?"

No answer.

Did he dare open that door? She could still be asleep, and she wouldn't take kindly to finding him in that bedroom.

And if she'd slept in nothing more than that shirt, if she'd kicked off the sheet and the blanket while she'd slept, it was no telling what he might see.

No, he decided, he didn't dare open that door.

He knew, once he reached the top of the steps that he didn't need to. He could hear her humming in the kitchen. He could smell the coffee as he got closer, and he could smell something else, as well—something sweet.

She'd gone out, and he should have cautioned her about that. He'd rather she didn't go anywhere by herself until this whole thing was settled. He was planning to do that, until he saw her standing there in his kitchen.

It was cinnamon that he'd smelled—a sticky, sweet cinnamon bun. She would find that specialty shop around the block. With her sweet tooth, it was a wonder the woman didn't weigh a hundred and fifty pounds.

But she didn't. She was a tiny little thing. Brian caught her standing in his kitchen, licking the gooey icing off her fingers, and he couldn't have looked away if his very life depended on it.

He hadn't known it was possible for a man to become so painfully aroused, so quickly, as he did while watching her lick that stuff off her fingers. He remembered the way he'd kissed his way across her lips, licking them clean for her, the day before.

"Holy, hell," he muttered, rooted to the spot. He couldn't leave. There was no way he could tear himself away from the sight of her now. And there was damned little he could hide from her while he was wearing nothing but these thin cotton pajamas.

Shelly, with one sticky finger still tucked between her lips, turned to face him.

"You didn't tell me you had one of those cinnamon bun places right around the corner from your house," she said lightly.

She was still wearing his shirt, only now it was tucked into the waistband of her jeans. She looked good in his shirt. He knew she would, and he was having trouble speaking.

"It was going to be my last resort," he said finally. "If nothing else worked, I was going to bribe you with that to get you to spend the night."

"It would have worked," she said. "These are great. I got you one, too."

Brian wondered what she'd say if she knew he'd lost his taste for sweets ages ago. At least, he had until yesterday. Nothing had ever tasted so sweet to him as she had.

"Thanks, but I think I'll pass," he said, heading for the coffee instead, hoping a jolt of caffeine would help clear his head.

She looked good in the morning with no makeup and her hair trying to escape from her braid so that little strands of it could curl around her pretty face. She was a very pretty woman. Not an elegant one, not a polished one, not a showy one. She looked a little innocent, a little naive, a little untouched.

But he had touched her. It wasn't much more than a hazy impression in his mind—much like that of a dream—but he had touched her.

He wanted to touch her again. Brian gulped the coffee instead, even though it didn't seem to be helping him.

"Sure you don't want this?" Shelly said, offering him one of those sticky buns.

He could only shake his head back and forth.

She tore off a piece of it, then set the rest down in the box. Brian watched every move she made as she ate it, and he started to sweat, here in his own kitchen, with this woman he'd known forever.

It didn't take her that long to finish it, and he was lucky this time. She rinsed her hands in the sink, dried them on a paper towel and dabbed at her mouth with it.

He wondered if she'd gotten all the icing off, and he wished he could have done that for her.

"These things are so messy," she said. He argued with himself about whether she knew what she was doing to him. He wondered what she had on under that shirt, wondered what she'd looked like when she'd been asleep in it in the bed across the hall from him.

He'd wondered about that long into the night.

And he wondered if her lips would taste as sweet this morning as they had the morning before. He didn't see how he could get through the day without finding the answer to that question.

"Brian?" she said. "What's wrong?"

What was wrong? He could make her a list. It might distract him from the things he really wanted to do to her. Then again, it probably wouldn't.

He wondered about the inevitability of certain things in life. He'd often felt as if the fates had fought a relentless battle to keep him and Rebecca apart—as if they simply weren't meant to be together.

He didn't like to think that way. He'd always felt he was in charge of his own life, that he could make it in to anything he wanted, that he could get whatever and whomever he wanted if he tried hard enough.

But maybe he couldn't. Maybe it was fate. Maybe it was inevitable that he couldn't be with Rebecca because he was meant to be with someone else. Maybe the woman was standing right there in front of him at that very moment—maybe she was the one.

Maybe he could have stopped himself from touching her then. Maybe he could have stopped the sun from setting that night.

He doubted it, even as he took that first step toward her.

"Brian?" She was worried now, and as he came forward she took a step backward. But she didn't make it very far. The island that stood in the middle of his kitchen, with the grill-top stove on the surface and the pots and pans hanging above kept her from getting too far away from him.

"Just give me a minute," he pleaded with her as he caught her face in his hands.

The fingers of his left hand fanned out across her cheekbones and settled into her hair. With his right hand, he traced the bones in her face, marveling at the smooth, soft skin.

He stroked her cheek, and she turned her face ever so slightly into his, welcoming his touch. She drew in a long, ragged breath, and her breasts rose in time with the air filling her lungs.

He couldn't help but watch, couldn't help but wonder what lay below the shadowy hollow beneath the open collar of that shirt.

She gasped for air again, bringing the tips of her breasts within a centimeter of brushing against his bare chest.

If he moved just a fraction, he could feel the weight of them against him. A button or two, a bit of cotton pulled down over her shoulders, and he could feel them pressed against his bare skin.

Shelly's lips parted on a sigh. He doubted she was even aware of the silent invitation, but he was. And it reminded him of why he'd started this in the first place.

Her lips, sticky sweet from that damned pastry—he wanted to taste them again.

Instead, because he needed to prove to himself that he still had an ounce of restraint left in his body, he traced her full lower lip with his thumb, then moved on to the upper one. They were soft and warm and open to him.

"Tell me to stop," he whispered, never taking his eyes off those lips. "And I will."

He'd find a way. It might well kill him, but he'd do it, if she asked him.

He waited for what seemed like an eternity. She hesitated, just long enough that he felt he had her consent, that he could touch his lips to hers with a reasonably clear conscience.

And he did.

It was a battle to keep from hauling her into his arms, grinding his lower body into the soft, warm welcoming heat he knew he'd find in hers, but he managed. He didn't see how, but he settled for bending his head and tasting her lips, stroking them with his tongue in short, light strokes, moving ever so slowly from one corner of her mouth to the other.

She trembled beneath his hands. Her breath caught in her throat, and her lashes fluttered downward. He kissed them, too.

He kissed her soft cheeks, and wished he'd been there to kiss away the tears he knew must have fallen that night in Tallahassee when he'd so callously taken what she'd offered him. He wished he could have kissed away the ache he'd known had taken root in her heart over the years when she must have wanted things from him that he hadn't even imagined.

He wished he could have kissed it all away, erased it all clean so they could have started with no shared past and nothing between them, including his promises not to touch her again until he was sure he knew what he wanted from her.

But he couldn't do that. He kissed her soft, sweet lips one more time before he made himself pull away, only to take her by the shoulders and hold her there, his forehead bent down so that it rested against hers, while they both struggled to breathe again. He was searching for something, for anything, he could tell her to explain what he was feeling. He just didn't know. The blatant desire was so strong it was blinding him to anything else.

And that was unlike him. He wasn't a man who got so caught up in wanting a woman that it pushed every other thought out of his head. He wanted to know a woman, to like her, to feel comfortable with her, before a relationship turned sexual. He'd learned a long time ago that a woman who could turn on his body wasn't necessarily one who could turn on his mind, as well. And one without the other fell far short of satisfying him.

He looked Shelly up and down again, looked over her flushed cheeks, her soft, sexy mouth, her downcast eyes.

He could hurt her so very easily. He knew that, and he'd already sworn to her and to himself that he wouldn't do that again.

Brian looked around this huge, empty kitchen, the one he'd picked with another woman in mind—Rebecca—one who'd never been here before and never would be. He couldn't help but compare the two women and what he felt for each of them.

He'd known it was over between him and Rebecca long before either of them had admitted it to the other. And as he tried now to reach back inside himself to what he'd felt for her and what he'd dreamed of finding with her, he couldn't do it.

It was like trying to grab a handful of the fog that rolled in across the beach in the mornings. He could see the cloudlike mist, but he couldn't hold it in his hand. He knew in his mind what it had been like to love Rebecca for all those years, but he couldn't feel it—not anymore.

Strange how far he'd come from it all in so short a time.

But what was he moving toward? What was he looking for with Shelly? What had he discovered between them?

He didn't know. He just knew that he wanted to know more about it. He wanted to explore this tangle of emotions between them, as much as he wanted to explore every inch of her beautiful body. And he had no right to do that now, when his head was so messed up, when she was so vulnerable to him.

He remembered how he'd felt, sitting on that plane beside her, coming back from Tallahassee. He remembered how much she'd been hurting and how little he'd been able to do to help her. He remembered thinking that if another man had hurt her like that, he would have wanted to kill the man.

He was going to have to be the one to take care of her now, to try in some way to make up for what he had done before today. This time, he'd have to protect her from himself.

"Shelly, I wish there was—"

His phone rang—thankfully. He didn't have any idea what he was going to say to her or how he could possibly explain his behavior.

"Hello," he said, grabbing the phone on the counter.

The conversation was short and simple. It was the police. They'd connected Charlie's name with an address they were called to this morning, and they thought Brian should come.

"Damn," Brian said. "I'll be there in fifteen minutes."

He ran a hand through his hair, then made a fist and wished he could slam it into one of the cabinets. When was this going to stop?

"What's wrong now?" Shelly said.

"We should have thought of that," he said, shaking his head. He knew exactly why he hadn't thought of it first. He'd been thinking of her instead.

"What?" She looked at him for the first time since he let her go.

He felt like a heel. "Somebody broke into Charlie's house, either yesterday or this morning. One of the neighbors called the police around nine this morning. The damned front door was hanging open."

"Let me guess," Shelly said. "His financial records? His business papers? They're gone?"

"I'm sure they are, but we need to go by there and check, anyway. There may be something there that the man missed. Damn," he said, downing his coffee in one big gulp. "We should have thought of it. We should have been there yesterday, after we found that mess at the office, and cleared all his stuff out of there."

"Wait a minute," she said. "We still have the stuff we got out last night—all those papers I took to my apartment."

"I hope we still have them," he said. "I think we'd better go to your apartment first and get that. Give me five minutes to shower and get dressed. Then we'll go."

She nodded, her cheeks still flushed, her eyes reluctantly meeting his.

Yeah, he felt like a heel. And he remembered that just before the phone rang he'd been trying to think of something, anything, he could say to her to explain it all.

He still hadn't thought of a thing.

"Look," he said, struggling for all he was worth, knowing he had to say something, "about what just happened here..."

"Let me guess," Shelly said, getting better all the time at hiding her own thoughts from him. "You still don't understand any of this."

"No." If he had nothing else to give her, it would be his honesty. "Do you?"

She shook her head, then turned to her side, subtly shutting him out.

He hated that feeling of being closed off from her. Brian turned her to face him with nothing but two fingers on her chin.

"But this time, there was no doubt in my mind about which woman I wanted or which one I was holding in my arms."

Granted, it wasn't much to give a woman. She had a right to expect that in the very least. But it was all he had right now. He didn't think she wanted to hear that he was half out of his mind from wanting her. And that was the only thing he was certain of right now.

Shelly didn't think she could stand to be in the house with him for one more night. Maybe not even for another hour. She punched in the security code, disabling the alarm so she could go outside.

Just standing in the driveway, staring at this huge house of his, was enough to make her feel a little better. Anything to get out of that kitchen.

He went upstairs to get dressed. Please, she prayed, let the man get dressed. Not that it would help much. Now that she'd seen him like that, she wasn't going to forget anytime soon.

Brian in nothing but a thin pair of pajama bottoms, hanging low and loose across his hips, his chest bare, his hand raking its way through his thick, dark hair.

This was what he'd look like if they spent the night together. If they'd made love, then wandered into the kitchen the next morning looking for coffee. That was exactly what he'd look like. Sexy as sin, rumpled, his body still warm from the bed, his eyes watching her, still remembering the way it had been the night before....

Oh, yes. She could see it now.

Shelly looked around the neighborhood of big stone houses painted in those washed-out pastels for which Naples was known. They sprawled over their oversize lots, topped by those distinctive reddish-colored tile roofs.

She wandered into the backyard, then to the canal that ran along the back of it. They were only a few blocks from the ocean, and she could smell it in the air.

He had picked an older neighborhood, one that for the most part had escaped the attention of the tourists, one that was filled with well-to-do people who actually lived and worked in Naples.

She could see him living here, but she couldn't see herself in a place like this. Not that he'd asked her to live here with him. Not that it was likely to happen anytime soon.

She couldn't let herself get carried away by nothing more than a couple of kisses and one colossal mistake in judgment on her part. It was crazy the way it had all changed so quickly. Nothing made sense anymore. Nothing was as it should be.

The world as she knew it seemed to have shifted beneath her feet, tilted on its axis, and in the course of less than two weeks everything had changed.

The way he'd watched her this morning. The way he'd touched her—gently, as always, but... differently.

He'd wanted to touch her, wanted that badly. He was fighting himself now; she recognized that in him so easily. For years, she'd been the one fighting against herself and her own desperate need to touch him, the way a woman touches a man.

And when he'd kissed her—she wasn't even sure she could call it that, though it had been more devastating than any real kiss she'd ever gotten. The way he'd run his lips across hers so carefully, so lightly, never daring to deepen the kiss. It was as if he were the one afraid of where that might lead.

He'd wanted her this morning. She'd been sure of that. She'd felt the yearning in his touch, felt that all-powerful combination of want and need that rationality couldn't explain away.

But why now? She couldn't help but wonder. Why now when she was more vulnerable to him than ever before?

She couldn't help but worry, either, that it was all tied up in him losing Rebecca. It had only been a week. Of course, he would have to have known for a while before that, but still . . . the wedding, the finality of it all.

It had only been one week. . . .

Shelly stood in the yard, savoring the solitude and the silence.

How she'd longed to be alone, to hide out with her insecurities and her illusions, to let them battle it out with her hopes and dreams to see which side won.

She wanted to be with him again. She wanted to throw herself into his arms and give him the kind of kiss he'd wanted to give her this morning. That was all it would take. They would have been in bed together in moments, if his conscience hadn't gotten in the way.

That was the only thing that had stopped her this morning. His conscience and her own insecurities.

Brian felt bad enough about the first time.

She'd be damned if she'd make love to him again only to have him feeling guilty as hell the next morning—again.

She didn't want his guilt. What she wanted was so much more than that.

Chapter 15

"You know," Brian said as they stood in the hallway outside her apartment fifteen minutes later, "if nothing else, the break-ins should be enough to convince the sheriff that he needs to look more closely into Charlie's death."

Shelly dug deep inside her purse for her new keys, coming up with them at last. "I still can't believe he's gone," she said, fitting the key into the lock. "And I need to go to the nursing home and tell them something about how Marion's bills are going to get paid. But I don't know..."

She broke off as the door swung open and she saw what was inside.

"Ahh!" She screamed, then clamped her hand over her mouth as she took a step back, right into Brian. "Oh, my God."

He caught her with a firm hand that slipped around her waist from behind. He pulled her back against the rock-solid wall of his chest, holding her up when her legs turned to mush.

Her apartment had been torn apart, just like the office, just like Charlie's house.

"Oh, my God." It was all she could say.

Shelly had known the situation was dangerous. If the near miss with the plane hadn't convinced her, Charlie's death had. But she'd never felt she was in danger herself. The plane crash hadn't been intended for her. She and Brian had just gotten in the way. They'd been in the wrong place at the wrong time.

But this? Someone had deliberately and calculatingly searched through all her things, leaving havoc behind. It looked as if a small child had thrown a temper tantrum here, with everything thrown this way and that.

"I can't believe this," she said, heading inside.

"Don't touch anything," Brian warned her. "The police may be able to find a fingerprint."

"This is insane. It's absolutely insane. Who would do something like this? What could they possibly want from here? What could Charlie have done to make someone so desperate?"

"I don't know," he said, taking her hand in his. "But we're going to find out. And we're going to stop him before anyone else gets hurt."

Once again, they found themselves tied up for most of the day with the police, both at Shelly's house and at Charlie's. The officers were much more interested in Grant Edwards's whereabouts. He was the only real lead they had. Brian wanted to know about the man, as well. He wanted to know if the man still meant anything to Shelly. He wondered why she still wore the man's shirt to bed.

He and Shelly salvaged what they could of Charlie's papers that she'd taken to her apartment. Whoever had been in her apartment hadn't taken anything else. He'd broken a few things, either because he'd been careless or because he'd been mad.

They spent hours at Charlie's, going through his things again. Whatever had been in those locked desk drawers was gone now, along with whatever Charlie had in the house pertaining to his own finances or the firm's.

How could they put this puzzle together when most of the pieces were missing? Brian wondered as they left the office, heading for Shelly's apartment so she could pack a bag to take to his house.

"When you were going through the things we took out of Charlie's house the first night, what did you find?"

"Mostly medical bills," she said. "Marion had an amazing number of medical bills."

"How much?" Brian asked. "More than he could pay?"

"No. That surprised me, actually. He'd paid them all—forty or fifty thousand dollars a year or more."

"How?" Brian asked. "How could he do that? That's sixty or seventy thousand dollars in earnings a year, before taxes, just for his wife's care. That's before he had anything for himself to live on. Was he making that kind of money with the business?"

"I don't know," Shelly said. "I never really got into that side of the business."

"It's a hell of a lot of money," Brian said. "Seems like there'd have to be a less expensive way of caring for his wife."

"Oh, there are. Marion wasn't always in the nursing home where she is now. Charlie put her in a less expensive place at first, but he wouldn't let her stay there."

"Why not?"

"You have to understand—Alzheimer's is so overwhelming, so devastating. She was like a child in many ways. She needed someone to watch her around the clock.

"The only reason Charlie put her in the nursing home to begin with was because she almost burned their house down one morning while Charlie was asleep. She was hungry, and she tried to cook herself some bacon. She forgot what she was doing and caught the house on fire.

"Charlie told me the first place he put her in just wasn't equipped to handle someone with her needs."

"What happened?"

Shelly remembered that day, when Charlie had finally come back to the office, and she'd been the only one still there. He'd been devastated when he'd explained it all to her.

"I guess they'd had a difficult time with Marion one day—she'd been really agitated and they couldn't calm her down. They were busy. There were other people who needed attention, too. So they'd put Marion in her wheelchair and tied her down to the chair.

"They must have left her that way for a while. She was hysterical when he got there, and she was taking some medication that upset her stomach. She'd thrown up all over herself, and they'd just left her there, tied to that chair."

"Good God," Brian said. "How could someone do that to the woman?"

"Unfortunately it's not that uncommon." Shelly had helped Charlie sort through everything as they searched for a new place to put his wife. She'd been amazed at what she'd found out about nursing homes. "There are a lot of places that rely on physical restraints to keep their patients from hurting themselves or from just wandering away.

"Anyway, Charlie had a fit about it. And he said then that he didn't care what it cost. He was going to get her into a private hospital that specialized in the care of Alzheimer's patients. He was never going to let anything like that happen to her again."

"You mean he was desperate," Brian said.

"No, that's not what I said. Charlie was a good man."

"I know," he said. "All I meant was the man needed a lot of money to take care of his wife. Desperation leads people to do things they wouldn't normally do."

Shelly shook her head. "What do you think he did?"

"Took a bribe, maybe."

"He wouldn't do that."

"He needed the money. He didn't have any insurance. The place costs thirty-five grand a year. You said yourself that he almost took the firm under when he was spending so much time taking care of his wife. Where was he going to get the money?"

"I don't believe he'd do anything like that."

"I know, Shel, but we've got to consider it. This firm is involved in some projects that run into a hundred million dollars or more. Charlie could help these clients with all the government inspection work he does."

"He wouldn't," she insisted.

"Think about it. Someone's cutting corners, saving themselves some money. They get the engineer inspecting the work to look the other way and they're home free."

"I just can't believe he'd do anything like that," Shelly said.

"I have trouble believing someone would want to kill him, but they did."

Shelly closed her eyes, remembering the man she'd known and trusted for years. He had loved his wife. He had been worried to death about how he was going to take care of her.

"Look," Brian said, taking her hand as they pulled into the parking lot of her apartment building. "I'm sorry. I know he meant a lot to you."

He was sorry he'd pushed her into thinking about all this. She'd been through enough that day without having to get into all of this. But he felt he was running out of time. He had to find out who was behind all this before someone came after Shelly.

Brian parked the car, but made no move to get out.

"When you looked over the financial stuff from his house, you said all the medical bills were paid. Where was the money coming from? Did you see any source for it? Did you see the tax records from the business? Was it bringing in that kind of money? Was he reporting that kind of income on his personal tax returns?"

"I don't know. I didn't get that far. I was still sorting through things that night when I decided to go to bed."

"Well then, that's a place we can start, at least. His banking records and his tax records. We know that the bank and the IRS have to have copies of those records," Brian said. "We can start there in the morning. We'll probably have to get the attorney to help us get access to them.

"Do you know who does his taxes?" he asked. "Or the firm's?"

"No, but I bet Maureen would. She looked after as much of Charlie's personal life as his business."

Brian checked his watch. It was only eight-thirty. "Do you know her home number?"

Shelly gave it to him, but reminded him that the intruder had pulled her phone jack out of the wall.

"I'll try them from here," he said, picking up the car phone. "The attorney, too. Then I'll be right up."

"I'm going to start packing."

Shelly fumbled with the keys the first time, then figured out what the problem was. Her hands were shaking. She was exhausted. She was mad. She was frightened. Her apartment had been trashed. A good friend of hers was dead, and

she was going to have to spend another night at Brian Sandelle's house.

She unlocked the door and stepped inside, closing it behind her. She threw her keys down on the kitchen counter.
She couldn't believe someone had done this to her apartment, that some stranger had pawed through everything she
owned.

Shelly shivered as she clicked on the light in the living
room and, cowardly as the thought was, she wished she'd
waited for Brian before she'd come inside. She didn't quite
feel safe here now. Everything was still out of place. She
hadn't taken the time to put the apartment back together. So
the place had taken on an unfamiliar appearance. She didn't
recognize it as her own anymore.

And there was a sinister feel about it, as if the man who'd
searched so recklessly had left something of his presence
behind to haunt her, to keep her from forgetting that he'd
been here.

He needn't have gone to that much trouble. She wasn't
likely to forget, not for a long time to come.

He knew where she lived.

He must think she had something of Charlie's that he
needed desperately.

Picking up her keys and turning to go, to wait for Brian
to come up here with her, she nearly walked right into the
man standing in the hallway, the man between her and the
front door—the only way out of her apartment.

"Ahh!" She didn't scream. She couldn't have gotten that
much of a sound out of her lungs. Everything simply froze
up inside her.

"Shh," the man in the shadows said, coming toward her,
coming into the light.

"Grant? Oh, my God, you scared me," she said, even as she started to back away from him. "What are you doing here?"

In her apartment? She had trouble believing that. He must have broken in. She wondered if he was the one who'd created the whole mess here, and the one at the firm, as well.

Surely not, she told herself, trying to remain calm. He'd tried to warn her away.

But still, he was here. He must have broken in.

"Did you hear about Charlie?" she said, thinking that maybe she could get him talking to her. All she had to do was keep him distracted for a few moments until Brian got here, and then... She didn't want to think about what might happen then. But at least there would be two of them and one of him.

He looked bad, Shelly thought. She hardly recognized him, he'd changed so much. He looked like a man who hadn't slept, showered or shaved in days. And he had this wild look in his eyes, a desperate, frightening look.

Where had he been? What had he done? What was he capable of doing?

"Charlie's dead, Grant," she said, making herself go on, forcing the thoughts through a brain that threatened to lock up on her.

She couldn't let that happen. Physically, she was no match for Grant Edwards. But mentally? She figured the field was fairly even on that score.

And she knew that a woman's best weapon against a man was her brain. She had to think. She had to do something. What?

And then Shelly got a wonderful idea about how she could distract him.

"I can't believe Charlie's..." She let her voice catch on a big, audible sigh and let herself think of all that had happened to her in the past week.

Next, she turned on the tears, letting them pour out like water dripping from a faucet. "I can't believe he's gone."

She didn't have to fake the trembling tone, the trembling in her body, but it took all the determination she had in her and all the acting skills she possessed to walk toward the menacing-looking man and sob a few times—all but inviting him to take her in his arms.

Shelly hid her face against the man's shoulder, grimacing in revulsion now that he couldn't see. It was a good plan, she thought. And if it wasn't, then it was all she could think to do at this moment, and she had to do something.

Just a few moments, she told herself. Brian would be here, and between the two of them they could handle Grant Edwards.

He stood stiffly beside her with his arms encircling her lightly. She could feel something hard and heavy in his pants.

Either he was getting off on this or he had a gun in his pocket.

A shiver ran through her body, but that was all right. It fit with the image she was trying to create. She sobbed a little louder.

"I just...can't...believe it," she said.

"What happened to him?" Grant asked cautiously. "The paper said it looked like he'd just gotten careless."

"Yes," she said, hoping if the tears didn't work, his fishing expedition would. She just needed a little more time. "It's so unlike Charlie to do something like that. But then..."

"What?" Grant was obviously eager for information.

"He hadn't been himself lately," Shelly said, still forcing herself to hang on to the man. If that was a gun in his pocket, he couldn't very well whip it out now, not with her plastered all over him. "Charlie had been behaving . . . a little strangely. He'd been so distracted."

"Really?"

"Yes. I think it's Marion. She's been much worse lately, and I think Charlie had been worrying about her a lot. Maybe that's all it was that day . . . the day he fell from that bridge."

"Yeah," Grant said, latching on to her explanation.

"It only takes a minute up there, one wrong move, one slip. . . ."

"Exactly," Grant said.

Shelly started sobbing all over again, clinging to him. He'd have to peel her off of him to get to that gun in his pants pocket.

She heard a clicking sound—a lock slipping into place in a door as it closed, she realized.

Grant heard it, too.

He pushed her away, but she held on, taking her time about moving away from him. She didn't want him making any sudden moves.

"I'm sorry," Brian said tightly. "The door was open and I . . ."

He looked from Grant to Shelly, then back again. And he didn't like what he saw. He didn't like it one bit.

Shelly almost smiled at the thought of Brian being jealous. She would have if she hadn't been so frightened. Brian was bigger than Grant was. He was stronger, most likely faster on his feet.

But Grant had a gun. She was sure of it now. And the gun more than evened the odds.

"I don't believe we've met," Brian said, extending a hand to the man standing warily beside her. "Brian Sandelle."

"Grant Edwards," he said, taking the hand that was offered him, then backing away to where Shelly stood. Grant put his arm around her and hauled her up against his side. "Shelly and I are old friends."

"So I see." Brian's jaw was clenched so tightly she was surprised he could get the words out. That was interesting, she decided.

Shelly took a step back and to the side, needing to warn Brian, who was watched her every move.

"Gun." She mouthed the word. Then, with her hand on the front, right pocket of her jeans, she showed Brian where it was.

"You lying little bitch," Grant said.

Shelly'd taken her eyes off him for too long. He lunged for her and his weapon at the same time. Grant was quick enough to catch Shelly. He held her in front of him in a choke hold with the gun drawn.

She found herself thrown off balance, his arm locked around her throat, half choking her as she struggled to get to her feet.

His gun was waving dangerously in the air, much too close to her head for her own liking. And Brian looked positively murderous.

"Back off," Grant barked at him.

Brian backed away, but he wasn't backing down. "You hurt her," he told Grant, "and I'll kill you myself."

Grant was breathing hard now, and Shelly was gasping for air against the pressure of the arm at her throat. She put her hands up to pull at his punishing arm, to claw at it. Grant only pulled his grip tighter, so tight she thought for a minute she was going to faint.

"You back off, too," he told her. "If you want to breathe, that is."

She could almost smell his fear, almost feel it hanging over the room.

She let her arms fall to her sides and managed to get her feet planted firmly on the floor, although it did her little good. He wasn't much taller than she was, and the way he was holding her she couldn't stand upright. He was deliberately holding her so low that it kept her off balance.

"What do you want, Grant?" she demanded, once she wasn't gasping for air. "What have you done?"

"I haven't done anything," he said.

"What about Charlie?"

"What about him? I didn't hurt him."

"Did you help him?" Brian said. "Did you help him find his way off that bridge?"

"He fell," Grant insisted, becoming more and more agitated. "The paper—it said he fell."

"But that's not what the sheriff thinks," Brian continued, never taking his eyes off Shelly. "He believes someone helped Charlie off that bridge, the same guy who bashed a rock over Charlie's head first, before he pushed him."

"I didn't do that," Grant said, sweating now. Shelly could smell him. "I didn't do any of that."

"The sheriff thinks you did," Brian said.

Shelly gasped as the gun swung away from her and toward the man she loved.

"Why would he think that?" Grant said. "Why would he know anything about me?"

"I told him," Shelly said, ignoring the warning look that Brian threw her. "I recognized your voice—on the phone. You tried to warn me away from here, didn't you, Grant?"

"What if I did? It doesn't mean that I... It doesn't mean anything," he insisted.

"The sheriff thinks it does," Brian said, drawing the man's wrath back to him.

Shelly couldn't stand it. She couldn't stand watching the gun pointed at Brian that way. She knew Grant. She didn't think he would hurt her, but she wasn't so sure about what he might do to Brian.

"You killed Charlie," she said, lashing out at Grant. "You cracked him over the head and then shoved him off that bridge."

Shelly couldn't see the look on his face, but she felt his panic. He was guilty as hell, she decided. "How could you do that to him? He was a good man, and I know the two of you were friends. How could you murder a friend?"

"It wasn't like that," he said with this wild look about him. "I never meant to hurt him. I just wanted to talk to him. I wanted to talk some sense into him, but he wouldn't listen to me."

"But you were there," Brian said. "You were with him that day on the bridge."

"What if I was?"

"You killed him," Shelly said, certain of it now. It made her feel absolutely sick inside. A man she knew, one she'd trusted, had killed Charlie.

"I'm telling you," he growled at her. "It wasn't like that."

"Why?" Brian asked. "Why did you do it. What are you after?"

"Look, I didn't mean to hurt anybody," he said, becoming more and more agitated. "He just . . . he wouldn't listen to me."

"You bastard," Shelly said. He killed Charlie, and now he had a gun in his hand pointed at Brian.

She wasn't going to give him a chance to use it. Shelly did the only thing she could think of to distract the man long enough for Brian to catch him off guard. She pretended to faint.

It wasn't hard. Her legs were like jelly, anyway. She let herself fall, throwing all her weight against the arm hooked around her neck. As she went down, she elbowed Grant in the stomach as hard as she could.

He groaned.

"Get down," Brian yelled to her as he dove into Grant, knocking him backward and following him to the floor.

They rolled together across the room, amidst the debris still littering the floor. Brian got his arm free, then took his clenched fist and shoved it into Grant's face, stunning him just long enough for Brian to get the gun away from him.

They both rose to their feet, breathing hard, watching each other warily.

"Get out of here, Shelly," Brian said, never taking his eyes off Grant. "Now! Go call the cops."

She should do that. She knew it. She was just having trouble convincing her legs to work. She'd been so scared.

"And you," Brian turned back to Grant. "You move a muscle, and I'll shoot."

Grant laughed, a dangerous, half-crazy sound. It sent a shiver up Shelly's spine.

"No, you won't," Grant said as he turned and fled, knocking Shelly down as he made his way to the front door and kept going.

Brian cursed and ran after him. He stopped in the doorway, extending his hands in front of him. He squeezed the trigger. Shelly braced herself for the big, booming sound, but heard nothing except Brian cursing for all he was worth.

He worked furiously over the unfamiliar gun for no more than an instant, then took aim again, too late. Grant had disappeared around the corner. Brian clicked a button on the back of the gun, then shoved it into his pocket in disgust.

"What happened?" Shelly said, the shock rolling over her now like waves that were breaking over her head, sucking her down, robbing her of the air she breathed.

Grant had been in her apartment, with a gun, pointed at Brian. She closed her eyes to the ugly images rushing through her head.

"Either he's stupid, he doesn't know his way around a gun or he never intended to shoot anyone—he still had the safety on the damned gun." Brian cursed under every ragged breath that left his body, cursed both himself and the man fleeing into the night.

Aw, hell, he thought, berating himself. He wasn't sure he could hit the guy, anyway, but he would have taken the shot. He could have done that, easily, because that man had held a gun to Shelly's head.

He could have shot him for that.

"Shel?" Brian said. Turning around, he saw her swaying on her feet.

He barely managed to catch her in time to keep her from hitting the floor.

Chapter 16

Shelly came to and found herself rocking and swaying, held tightly against Brian as he carried her down the hallway. She must have been out longer than she realized, because in a moment, they were outside, heading for his car.

She lifted her head off his shoulder and pushed against him slightly. She was ready for him to put her down, feeling foolish that he'd had to pick her up in the first place, but Brian would have nothing of that.

"Be still," he said, the tight control evident in his tone. "We're almost to the car."

Shelly found it hard to breathe again, just as she had when Grant's arm had tightened around her throat.

It was cool outside and pitch-black, the shadowy images spinning. Or was it her head that was spinning? She was more shaken than she'd realized.

Grant had had a gun, yet he hadn't been prepared to use it. But if he had, Brian would likely have shot him by now, and she suspected this whole mess would have been over.

Grant had been like a madman, a desperate, reckless, dangerous man. She had hardly recognized him.

She could still feel him crushing her throat, robbing her of the very air she breathed. She could see him waving that gun all over the place, then aiming it directly at Brian's heart.

Even though she knew now that he'd never taken off the safety catch on the gun, she went cold all over again.

They got to the car. Brian set her on her feet, but didn't let go of her.

"Hang on," he said, leaving her pressed against his side, between him and the car, while he found his keys and unlocked her door.

Shelly got in with his help, then let herself sink down into the seat. She let her head fall back against the headrest while she closed her eyes and tried not to think of what had happened up there.

She heard Brian get in beside her, punch out a number on his car phone, then explain the situation to what must have been an emergency dispatcher.

It didn't sound nearly as bad as it had felt. A man in her apartment with a gun, threatening them both, then fleeing into the night.... A man who was wanted for questioning in the suspicious death of their boss.

Grant could be anywhere, she thought, turning her head to the side and trying to figure out whether she saw anything moving outside. He could be in the shadows beside the building, in the next block, in the next county before too long. He could be anywhere at all.

They didn't even know what he wanted. They didn't know anything and—

"The police are coming," Brian said, sounding almost angry as he hung up the phone.

"He killed Charlie," she said.

"I know he did. Are you all right?"

Not trusting her voice, she nodded.

Brian couldn't see that. It was too dark in the car. Besides, he wanted to see for himself that she was all right. He flicked on the overhead light and looked down into her chalky-white face. She had dark circles under her eyes—lack of sleep, no doubt—the bruise on her cheekbone faint but still there.

She'd have new ones tomorrow, from where that bastard had grabbed her around her neck.

Brian felt positively violent when he thought of the way she'd tried to protect him. She'd drawn the man's attention—and the gun—away from him and back to her.

He would have admired her for her courage and her quick thinking if he hadn't been so damned mad at her for putting so little value on her own safety.

Just thinking about it had Brian curling his hand into a fist. He was angrier than he'd ever been in his life. Frightened, frustrated, confused, impatient—it all simmered there inside him, just begging for an excuse to get out.

Grant Edwards had given him an excuse and unwillingly given up his gun, as well.

Brian could have shot the man. He was that angry at him and that determined that the man never get a chance to hurt Shelly again.

When he thought about the risk she'd taken in there, he just saw red, but even as he wanted to lash out at her, he knew he couldn't.

It was the last thing she needed right now. And there was something he needed much more than that.

He slid his seat back as far as it would go and hauled Shelly across the console that separated them. He then sat her on his lap with her head tucked against his shoulder and his arms holding her tight. He didn't question anymore the way she felt in his arms, the way she fit there as if she'd been made to be held close to him.

She was trembling badly, her breath coming out in shaky little puffs. And she was cold to the touch.

Brian shifted her slightly in his arms, to press her more closely against him. He kissed her cheek, the corner of her eye, her forehead.

God, he'd needed to do this.

He didn't understand how a man's feelings for a woman could grow and change so much, so quickly. He didn't know how he was going to explain that to her, either. How he could possibly make her believe that what he felt for her now was real.

If they just had a little time together, without all this craziness, he would make her believe. He wouldn't give up until he did.

For now, for this moment, it was enough to hold her close. Again, like that time on the riverbank after the plane had gone down, he didn't see how he'd ever manage to let her go.

Shelly wriggled around, trying to sit up, trying to pull herself away from him, and it make him furious all over again.

"Don't even think about it," he said, locking his arms around her.

There was no way he was going to let her go.

They were still sitting there, just like that, when the sound of the sirens finally reached them.

When the police arrived, Brian and Shelly went over the basics of what happened while still in the parking lot. Then the police fanned out around the area to see if they could locate Grant Edwards.

There were more questions to answer for the officer who followed them back to Brian's house. The officer also wanted names and phone numbers of all the firm's employees so he could check on them, as well.

Shelly left in the midst of that, feeling as battered emotionally as she did physically. She took aspirin for her head, found some cough drops that she figured might help her sore throat and helped herself to the whirlpool tub in Brian's bathroom.

She was too tired to cry, too mixed up to even figure out what she might cry about if she had the energy. Besides, her head already hurt. Crying would only make it worse. She just soaked in the warm water until it turned cool enough to make her want to get out.

It wasn't until she'd dried off with a massive, dark green towel that she remembered she'd never gotten any clothes out of her apartment.

Since there was nothing else in the bathroom except the clothes she'd just taken off, Shelly put on the bathrobe that was hanging on the hook on the back of the bathroom door. It was green terry cloth, a mile too big for her, and, just her luck, it smelled of Brian. The scent enveloped her as completely as the robe did.

God, was she ever going to get out of this man's house? Out of his robes and his shirts and his life?

Would she ever stop reliving those stolen moments they'd spent together since this whole mess started? The precious few kisses they'd shared, the look in his eyes when he'd let her go this morning in the kitchen or the way his arms felt when they closed around her in the car tonight? Would she ever stop hoping? Stop wanting? Stop loving him?

She didn't see how. She didn't—

There was a knock on the bathroom door. "Shelly?"

She sat down on the edge of the big tub and let her face drop into her hands. Oh, how she wished she'd made it to the bed in the next room without having to face him again that night.

"Shel? You all right?" He knocked again.

"I'll be out in a minute," she managed to say, dreading the moment when she had to open that door.

She was simply at the end of her rope. She couldn't take any more of this, and she desperately wanted to be alone. She needed time to gather her defenses, to try to put back together that shield she'd always worn when he was around.

It was probably a lost cause. She knew that. But he'd already seen more than he needed to know of how she felt about him.

"Shelly? Open this door."

She swallowed hard, forced herself to rise and walk past the double marble vanity to the door. The lock turned with a small click, and she barely had time to step back before he opened the door and stepped in.

He'd unbuttoned his white dress shirt all the way and pulled the tail ends loose from his jeans, leaving bare a two-inch-wide strip of tanned, muscled chest and stomach.

"You all right?" he asked.

She nodded, barely.

He must have been getting undressed for bed when he heard her in here, she decided. Shelly closed her eyes at the image of him walking in here, shedding his clothes—all of them, she suspected—and climbing into that big bed in the room behind him.

Her cheeks burned at the thought—that and being caught staring at him—even if he was staring back at her.

He was as absolutely baffled by all this as she was. Shelly was certain of that. He could turn her insides to mush with one look, one oh-so-light touch.

He'd been quiet in the car on the drive back to his house, and he hadn't touched her at all. But now...now he just stood in front of her, watching her watch him, heating her blood with nothing but the look in his eyes.

He did want her. Shelly knew that. It was a sweet reward for all those years she'd wanted him, just to know that he wanted her now, as well.

Why he felt that way, she couldn't say. Curiosity? Sheer proximity? Standing in front of a man waving a loaded gun at them mere hours ago and wondering if they'd both come out of that alive? It could have been any of those things. None of them added up to a good reason to fall into bed with someone, though.

Loving him the way she did, wanting him as she did, knowing that he wanted her, too, that he cared for her deeply, even if it wasn't the kind of love she wanted—surely that was reason enough.

Surely it was, she told herself, while at the same time acknowledging that she still had her doubts.

It might make it harder, in the end, when it came time to leave him. Shelly knew most likely the time was coming when she'd have to leave him, for her own sake. And being intimate with him again would only make it harder for her.

But, she reasoned with herself, how much harder could it be? How much clearer could the memories she had of him be? They couldn't be any clearer. They were etched into the surface of her brain.

She would never forget him, never truly escape him.

So why couldn't they have this one night together? One she'd always dreamed of? One he'd cheated her out of before, when he'd been dreaming of someone else?

That thought, and that alone, gave her pause when nothing else could have. She would not be a substitute for the woman he really loved.

Shelly found the courage then to look him in the eye.

He stood like a statute, not moving, barely breathing, his hands clenched tightly to his sides.

He was angry, she thought at first. But she'd believed that, too, at first, tonight in the car. He had been angry then, but there had been more to it. She hadn't figured out what it was, but there was more than anger there, and now she was seeing it again.

That was curious, she thought, taking one step closer to him, watching him pull himself up a little straighter, his chest filling with the air he took in, his shoulders seeming just a little broader as he braced himself.

Braced himself for what? she wondered.

Brian was fighting desperately for control and wondered if she realized it. "I thought you'd gone to bed," he said finally, as if that explained why he could do nothing but stand there and stare at her.

He wondered if she realized how she looked, standing in his bathroom—so soft, so pretty, and sexy as hell. Her hair was still dripping, her skin a little flushed. She was wearing nothing but his bathrobe.

He was certain—enough that his throat tightened painfully— that she wasn't wearing anything but that robe.

"Damn," he muttered. He tried to look away, but couldn't.

From the bedroom, he heard a clicking sound—the tape he'd turned on a moment ago had finally run to the end of one side and switched to the beginning of the other—then the sound of a soft, sexy saxophone playing mournfully in the background.

He knew he'd recognized the music that had been playing that night in the hotel in Tallahassee—the song they'd danced to, the one they'd made love to.

Sometimes, when torturing himself didn't seem like such a bad idea, he played it here at night. When he couldn't sleep, and he let himself think of her and the way she'd felt in his arms that night.

He watched her now and waited, wanting her all the more, thinking of her, soft and wet and naked inside that robe of his. He didn't see how he'd ever be able to wear it again without thinking of her in it.

The music rose higher, the melody distinctive and mournful. She recognized the song. He could tell by the way her chin came up just a fraction as she tried not to let him see that it bothered her to hear that song now with him.

The tension in the room kicked up another notch, past the point of being unbearable, right into the stratosphere as far as he was concerned.

She wasn't a foot away from him, less than the length of his arm. All he had to do was lift his arms from his sides and hold them out to her. He could have her in his arms in a fraction of a second.

And then he'd be lost.

He was a man who prided himself on his self-control, his ability to think things through and to act on logic and reason rather than emotion. She'd robbed him of that, though he couldn't say he regretted what she'd done to him.

A woman he'd known for years, one he'd protected and looked out for and loved like a sister—she'd done this to him. She'd turned him inside out. She had him at the brink of breaking a vow he'd made to her and himself—that he wouldn't ever hurt her again and that he wouldn't come to her until he was sure of his feelings for her.

And right now there was so damned little he could be sure of.

That he wanted her so much he ached with it. That he was scared to death of losing her and determined to protect her in each and every way, even from himself. Those two things were all he could say for certain, and it wasn't enough—not for her.

But it was enough to keep him from closing the distance between them and hauling her into his arms. Because if he did, he'd never be able to let her go without making love to her.

He shook his head and threw up his hands, disgusted with himself and his own lack of control, but he didn't back away.

"I thought you'd gone to bed," he said again, trying to pry his eyes off her. "I thought all I'd have to do was make it past that closed door of the bedroom where you were sleeping. Thought I might actually be exhausted enough to sleep tonight. And even if I did dream about you again... You did know I've been dreaming of you?"

"No," she whispered, pulling the robe tighter around her, cutting off his view of that distinctive, shadowy hollow between her breasts, reminding him again of that awful, wonderful night they'd spent together.

He remembered the way he'd nestled his face against her sweet-smelling hair only moments before he'd fallen to his knees in front of her and buried his face in that space between her breasts.

They were so perfect, so sexy. He remembered the slight weight of them against his hand. Did he remember the way they'd tasted, as well? He thought he did.

Brian groaned again.

She was remembering, too. He knew it in some unexplainable, elemental way. And despite what he'd done to her before, she still wanted him.

He was infinitely grateful for that, even as he fought against the desire that rose so potently between them. Like a force field, it surrounded them. Like something that had its own mysterious source of energy, one that grew instead of lessened with time, it tightened its hold on them yet again.

"I do," he admitted. "I dream about you every night. And I thought the dreaming might be enough. I thought if I could walk past your door, I might make it till morning before I put my hands on you again." And with that, he took the first step. He took her hand in his and ran his thumb across the back of it.

Touching her at last, even in this small, simple way, was such a relief. He'd wanted this so badly, needed it more than he needed his next breath.

She was warm to the touch, and her hand was trembling. Or maybe it was his hand. Maybe they both were.

Brian realized it had been years since she'd touched him voluntarily. It used to come easily between them. A quick hug. A friendly kiss on the cheek. But it wasn't that way now. She went out of her way to avoid touching him in the smallest of ways. And he found himself wanting her touch, needing it.

He tugged on her hand, slipping it inside the ends of his shirt and pressing her palm to his chest, right over his racing heart. With his hand over hers, he held it there, wanting her to feel for herself what she'd done to him.

"I get up every morning," he told her, "hoping I can make it one more day without laying my hands on you, yet hoping at the same time that I won't. Because I know that once I let myself touch you, I'll have to pry my hands off of you."

And that's what it was going to take tonight—prying his hands off of her. He could do it. He would, if she asked him to. He found himself praying that she wouldn't ask.

He allowed himself one step to bring his body closer to hers. Another, and her soft breasts would be nestled against his chest. All it would take was a tug on the belt of that robe, a swipe of his hands to pull the ends apart, and he would have her right there, her skin to his, her heart pressed against his.

But he didn't do that. He didn't make that move yet. He stopped once again, this time to wonder exactly what was in her heart.

He knew she had loved him once, through no encouragement from him and, due to his longtime involvement with Rebecca, with little hope that they might have a future together. And he knew that he must have hurt her over and over again. He swore silently, just remembering all the times he'd turned to her, his friend, his confidante, when he needed someone to talk to about whatever problem he and Rebecca were having at the time.

That had to hurt in ways he couldn't imagine. And he wondered how much of her feelings for him had survived that and the events of that fateful weekend in Tallahassee with him.

"I don't want to hurt you," he said.

And he would hold that thought uppermost in his mind, far above the way his body yearned for her.

He would not hurt her again.

Her pretty brown eyes collided with his. It was the first time she'd looked him in the eye since he'd come into the bathroom. Was she scared? That part was easy enough to see. But the rest of it—he couldn't say.

"What do you want?" she said finally.

Brian breathed a little easier then. That part was easy. "You," he said, letting himself take that last step, to settle his body flush against hers. "In my bed, tonight. Only you."

It was a little like skimming along atop a live wire, he thought. The power was racing between them, the voltage dangerously high, the possibility of being burned ever present. One wrong move and it could all turn to ashes.

He didn't want to frighten her. He wouldn't allow himself to push her or to pressure her—a fine line he didn't think he'd crossed just yet. But he was coming treacherously close to his own breaking point. The sweat beaded on his skin. His hands settled onto her arms, and she was swaying on her feet, coming closer one moment, easing away the next.

The saxophone mourned on, the beat becoming hypnotic. He could imagine picking up the beat himself, thrusting into her in time to the music.

He'd done that—that night. But he didn't do it now.

Not yet.

If she'd been anyone else, he would have promised her he'd make it good for her, that he wouldn't stop until she was burning up inside for wanting him, just as he was burning alive wanting her.

But the two of them were long past the point of worrying about satisfying a physical need. It went much deeper than that. He hoped she knew that. He needed to try to explain it to her, but he wasn't sure he could put all the words together in his head to do that just now.

He pulled her a fraction of an inch closer, gently thrusting his painfully aroused body against hers, showing her this time, rather than telling her, exactly how much he wanted her.

Her lips parted, her breath coming out in a rush. It reminded him of the way it had felt, taking nothing but the smallest, sweetest taste of her earlier in the day.

A taste wouldn't do it now. He was ravenous. Like a starving man, he wanted to devour her. He wanted to feast on her body and reach clear down to her soul, to touch it with his own. He wanted to take all of her, to see all of her, to make her a part of him and to become a part of her.

He wanted all of that.

But he took only a taste of her lips, one brief touch of his lips to hers, one brief glimpse of the pure passion smoldering between them. They could go up in flames at any moment, this wildfire spiraling out of control.

He was dangerously close to losing control.

"Tell me what you want," he said, before he lost it all. "I need to hear you say it. I need to know that you want me as much as I want you."

"I do..." she said, hesitating. Shelly knew there would be no miraculous admissions of love from him, not tonight, probably not ever.

She was being foolish to hold out for any such declaration. Brian wouldn't dream of saying such a thing to her if he didn't mean every word of it.

And he didn't love her.

It didn't hurt quite as much as she remembered. At one time, it had been absolutely devastating. Maybe she'd learned to live with it, after all. Maybe knowing how much he desired her, if only at this moment, helped in some small way to make up for the lack of his love.

She'd won much more than some inconsequential admission of desire from him. They wouldn't have come this far if that was all it was.

Women had been falling all over him for years, and if all he'd wanted was a woman, he would have found another one, one who wanted nothing more than to satisfy a physical need rather than an emotional one.

He knew that she loved him. He wasn't a man who toyed with a woman; she knew he wouldn't have been here if nothing more than desire was involved.

But he did want her. He wanted her desperately. She watched him at war with himself, watched the way the muscles in his arms were clenched tight while the hands that held her were made gentle by nothing more than the force of his determination to make them so.

He would let her go, even now, if that's what she wanted.

She didn't see how she could ever escape this awful push and pull inside her, between what she wanted from him and what he was offering her tonight. But like him, she also didn't see how she could pry her body apart from his in this moment.

"I do want you," she said. "I always have."

"And that's enough?" he asked urgently, his lips a breath away from hers, ready and more than willing, more than eager to cross the final barrier. "For tonight? That's enough?"

"Yes."

They never made it to the bed. At least, not the first time. Shelly simply melted against him, suddenly breathless, boneless, bloodless.

It was like being on fire, she imagined. Scorching hot, glowing with a blinding light, consuming her entire being, robbing her of the ability to move or to think. She lost all but the vaguest recollections of the world around her. The robe, his robe, that they almost didn't get off of her because it meant letting go of each other for a moment. The cool edge of the marble as he sat her on top of it, the slickness of the steamed mirror at her back. Brian watching her reflection in it, telling her how beautiful she looked with her body wrapped around his.

Greedily, she wanted him right then, and she wanted forever.

She settled for the one night.

His body, tall and sleek and hard, against her and inside her. His mouth, a lifeline she couldn't get enough of. His arms around her, sure and strong, fitting her to the slow, sweet, tormenting rhythm of his, matched to the sound of the wailing saxophone—she remembered it all.

She remembered begging him, pleading with him, to let it end, before she surely died from the pleasure, but he didn't. He teased her unmercifully, taking her right to the edge, then backing down again, back and forth, again and again. He took her one step closer each time, pushed her ever higher into her own spiraling, aching need.

It was madness, she realized in some corner of her mind as she clung desperately to the smooth skin of his bare bottom. It was impossible, but she wanted him closer, wanted him deeper inside her until the lines between them merged and there was no more of him, no more of her, only the magic that was the two of them.

And as he finally gave in, that maddening self-control of his finally shattered. His eyes were blazing down into hers, his body and hers giving way to a passion that would no longer be denied.

"Only you," he whispered then, and later, when he carried her to bed and loved her all over again. "Only you."

Chapter 17

The bed carried this wonderfully musky smell of Brian, and Shelly wished she could stay there, the night never ending. She found a spot to the left side of the big bed that still held the warmth of his body, and she rolled into it.

Obviously he hadn't been up long.

Shelly felt a shiver work its way down her spine, an unsettling mixture of pleasure and fear. If she couldn't make the night last forever, it meant she had to face him in the light of day, and she didn't want to do that. She wanted to hide somewhere, alone, and try to figure out what the night before had meant, both to her and to him.

A blush rose in her cheeks at the image flitting through her mind from the wonderful, seemingly endless night that had passed. He hadn't said that he loved her, but he'd taken her with love and a passion she'd never experienced before, never even imagined.

The doubting side of her wondered if he'd worked so hard to show her how great his desire for her was to make up for the fact that she wanted so much more that he couldn't give her.

He would do that, if he knew how much she wanted the words he couldn't say. He would give her all he could to somehow make up for that.

But she knew that, above all, he would give her his honesty. He hadn't said he loved her, because he didn't. Having him make love to her would have to be enough, for now, probably forever.

She wouldn't be sorry for that. She couldn't be. The night had meant too much to her, and the memories would be too precious to allow any regrets she might have to spoil them.

He had been a demanding lover and a generous one. A tireless, passionate, sexy man who made it quite clear to her that he would gladly do anything to please her.

And he had.

Shelly opened her eyes and glanced around the room. There was no sound coming from the bathroom, so he'd probably gone downstairs already. Sunlight was coming in through the blinds, and the clock on the nightstand read 8:10, late for her and for him.

Much as she'd love to linger here in this bed, she had to get up. She had to face Brian, get on with her life. There was work to be done, Charlie's company to be put back together, his killer caught, his wife provided for somehow.

Once that was done... Who's to say what would happen then?

Shelly finally came downstairs wearing her snug jeans and a man's shirt.

Brian didn't think it would be such a good idea to demand to know whether or not it was his shirt, although he liked the idea of her digging around in his closet, looking for something to wear. He'd wanted to go back upstairs and wake her with a kiss, wanted to make love to her just one more time as she came awake, before she had time to think too much about all that had passed between them.

The complications, the uncertainties, the fears, had faded into the night, the passion overcoming them. That wouldn't be the case in the bright light of day.

He should have been back in that bed with her hours ago; he figured it would be a while before he got her back there again. And he wanted her back in his bed. Being with her hadn't lessened his desire for her in the least. If anything, it had only heightened it. They'd found a rare and wondrous thing between them.

"Good morning," he said. He stayed where he was, though he'd rather have been by her side. When she'd come downstairs, she'd hesitated, just inside the doorway, without even coming into the kitchen. And in that moment, she looked both very young and very uncertain.

Despite the fact that she'd come to him of her own accord the night before, he still felt more than a twinge of guilt about it all. He'd pushed her, even if he'd barely touched her. He'd pushed more than he had a right to do. He'd wanted her so desperately. Though he wanted very much to go to her and to take her into his arms now, he wasn't sure how she'd take that. He was afraid of where it might lead.

He didn't know if he could do what needed to be done right now if he started out with her in his arms.

She was going to be angry enough with him before the morning was over.

He'd come to some decisions a few hours ago, once he'd managed to pry his thoughts away from the night they'd shared. And she wasn't going to like them.

"You all right?" he asked, wanting to tell her a thousand things other than what he was about to say.

She nodded.

Time was running out, he noted as he glanced at his watch.

"I don't have much time. I have an appointment with Charlie's lawyer to see if we can get the tax records out of the IRS and the banking records."

"Oh." She hesitated, still not budging from the doorway.

"You don't have much time, either," he added.

"What?"

"There's a commuter flight leaving this morning at nine, with a connecting flight that'll take you to Tallahassee. I'd like you to be on it."

He watched while her complexion turned chalky, then realized this wasn't the way to start a morning-after conversation with a woman he'd made love to all night long.

"I want you to go to my parents' house," he said. "You'll be safe there until this whole thing is over."

She shook her head, her color a little better. "I'll be fine here."

"You can't promise me that any more than I can promise to protect you," he said, wanting more than a promise. He wanted a guarantee that she would be fine, and this was the only way he could think of to be sure of that.

"I never asked you to promise to protect me, and I—"

"But I thought I could, and I've been doing a damned poor job of it."

That got her back up, and Brian saw the conversation going downhill quickly.

"I'm not yours to protect," she said.

"Would you like to be?" he asked, stopping her cold.

She stiffened, her back ramrod straight. She crossed her arms in front of her chest and tilted her head to the side.

He saw clearly the bruises that Grant Edwards had left on her throat the night before. The sight of them didn't do anything to help him calm down, which he needed to do if he was going to talk her into getting the hell out of town.

"I want a lot of things right now," he told her, and knew that he should have started this conversation with her in his arms. "I could start listing them all, but I don't see how getting into that would solve anything."

Brian allowed himself one step toward her. When she didn't back away, he took another. "There are two things on top of my list, and they both concern you. First, I want you safe. Second, when this whole thing is over I want some time alone with you to figure out exactly what this thing between us is. Surely, we both deserve that."

"Yes," Shelly said when she could breathe again. "But that doesn't mean I have to leave town."

"I haven't slept in days," he admitted. "When I wasn't staying up nights trying to figure out who wanted to kill Charlie and who was after you, I was tossing and turning in that bed, going half out of my mind trying to remember just how it felt to be with you in that hotel room in Tallahassee."

She swallowed hard. She didn't want to say anything, to give anything away right then. It was spiteful of her, she knew, but she liked the image of him for once being the one to lose sleep over her, rather than the other way around.

"Shel, I can't think straight with you around, and if you stay, I won't let you out of my sight, so I'll never get anything done."

Well, she was so sorry about that, but resisted the urge to tell him. "I have some things I need to do myself," she reminded him instead. "I have responsibilities to Charlie and his wife. He was a good friend, and he put a lot of trust in me. I can't walk away from all that he asked me to do for him."

"Let me take care of those things, just until the police find Grant Edwards and lock him away."

"And who's going to take care of you?"

He came a little closer, and at six-two he practically towered over her. "I'm bigger than you. I'm faster, and I'm stronger."

"Which isn't going to make a bit of difference if Grant has another gun."

"Come on, Shel. You know size and strength account for a lot, particularly when it's a man going up against a woman."

She didn't say anything. She couldn't. She didn't care for his idea that she was some helpless little girl in need of his protection. But she still remembered how powerless she'd felt the day before when Grant had hold of her. She might have gotten out of there by herself. It was possible.

"Shelly, there are a million different ways for a man to hurt a woman," he said. "I don't want you hurt."

"I know, I just—"

He silenced her with one finger that slid across her lips in a paralyzing caress. She shivered in spite of herself, knowing he'd only meant to quiet her, knowing it was becoming impossible to hide her reaction to his touch, something she did now out of habit rather than necessity.

Surely her reaction to him the night before had left no room for doubt about her feelings for him.

"Do you love me?" he asked, his words leaving her absolutely reeling.

This massive weight settled itself on top of her chest, making it hard to breathe, hard to move.

He couldn't be asking this of her, not now. He wouldn't back her into this kind of corner. It wasn't fair of him, and he was an extremely fair-minded man.

"Brian," she pleaded. She started trembling in earnest now, and she didn't see any way out of this.

He knew the answer already. She could see it in his eyes. And she thought he must have some ideas of his own about how he could make her admit it to him.

"Do you love me?"

She closed her eyes, praying this was nothing more than a dream, but opened them again and saw him still standing there. What was the use, she told herself. He already knew. "Yes," she said breathlessly. "I do."

She waited for the regrets to come, waited for the uneasiness to settle in between them. She'd always been sure that admitting her feelings to him would only make him uncomfortable.

But he wasn't. He didn't seem to be uncomfortable at all. If anything, he looked ridiculously pleased with himself, though he tried to hide it.

"Then do this for me," he said. "Do this, and I won't ask anything else of you."

"That's not fair," she said.

"I know. It's rotten of me, but I'm desperate. And that plane's leaving in an hour. I want you on it."

Shelly knew it was selfish of her, maybe even foolish, considering the danger, but she didn't want to be apart from him now. What if all they ever had was this time together? She didn't want to miss a single moment of it.

"That man is still out there, Shel. He was acting half-crazy last night, and there's no telling what he might do."

"I don't think he'd really hurt me."

"You don't?"

"No."

"C'm'ere," he said. He took her by the arm to the bathroom down the hall and flicked on the lights. He turned her toward the mirror, and he stood behind her. Pulling her hair aside, he showed her what he'd obviously already seen himself—two bluish gray bruises on the side of her throat.

"I was right there beside you, and he still managed to do this. Have you thought about what else he could have done? Because I have."

"He didn't even take the safety off the gun," she said, standing still beneath the hands that had settled against her shoulders and watching his reflection in the mirror.

"So? He could have been nervous. He could have thought he wouldn't have needed to shoot to get what he wanted from you. He might be just plain careless with a gun. That makes him even more dangerous."

He was massaging her shoulders now, his fingers and his thumbs running deep into the tension-filled muscles.

"Please leave," he said. "I reserved a ticket for you already. I'd take you to the airport myself, but I'm supposed to meet with the lawyer in fifteen minutes, and he has to be in court right after that. I'll call you a cab. You can buy some clothes when you get there, and my mother will be waiting for you at the airport, all right?"

Finally she gave in with a nod.

"Thank you," he said.

His arms closed around her from behind, locking them together across her chest. He pulled her back against him and squeezed her tightly, letting his warmth seep into her.

For the first time since she woke up alone, she didn't feel so uneasy about the night they'd shared.

"About last night," he said, closing his eyes. His face dropped into that hollow where her neck and shoulders met, his breath so warm it sent shivers shooting across the sensitive skin.

Her body reacted in an instant, her breasts full and aching, her legs turning to mush. Her body remembered everything about his.

"I don't think I can put it in to words," he whispered, his lips against her skin. "I could say it was incredible, but that doesn't begin to describe it."

Shelly swallowed hard. The relief was enormous. He didn't regret anything. And now she could hope that the night had meant as much to him as it did to her.

"I could say that I've never felt so close to another human being, so in tune with you. Yet as close as we were, it wasn't close enough," he said.

She stood there in his arms, shivering with pleasure, goose bumps rising on her flesh as he started kissing her again.

"I . . . I don't want to be away from you right now," she said when she could get the words out.

"Sweetheart, I don't want to be away from you, either, but I'm not taking any chances on this. I'm not going to lose you now."

In the end, she gathered up the few possessions she'd picked up at her apartment, stuffed them all in a small piece of his luggage and tried not to miss him already.

He'd dashed out the door only moments before, with time for nothing more than a single, breath-robbing kiss before he left.

As promised, she locked the door behind him and set the security system. Then she sat down to wait for the cab.

Brian had talked to the police already this morning. There was a warrant out for the arrest of Grant Edwards. The charge against him was murder, among other things.

They were sure it had all started with some kickbacks for looking the other way to a problem on some engineering job. They'd found a motive, too. Grant had gotten in over his head at the racetrack. He owed some local bookie about a hundred thousand dollars, from what the police had been able to find out.

The police were sure they would have Grant in custody within a few days. Obviously the man hadn't found whatever he was looking for either at the firm or Charlie's house or hers, because he was still looking for it. And it must have meant a great deal to him, enough that he was willing to pull a gun on her and Brian.

The police thought Grant Edwards was a desperate man, that he'd do something incredibly stupid very soon and they would catch him.

Shelly didn't expect to be out of town for long. She didn't want to go, but Brian had asked, and it was clearly very important to him. He'd talked about time—the time they deserved—to be together and to figure things out.

"I'm not taking any chances," he'd said. "I'm not going to lose you now."

She smiled as she remembered it. After he'd said that, she would have gone to the moon for the man.

Shelly heard what must have been the cab tooting its horn out front. She was turning to leave when the phone rang. She grabbed it while picking up her purse and her bag.

"Ms. Wilkerson?" a woman's voice said.

"Yes," Shelly said, relieved that Grant hadn't found her.

"This is Mrs. Thompson."

"Yes," she said, recognizing the woman's name from the nursing home.

"I hope it's all right to call you there. Your office gave me the number."

"Of course. Is something wrong?"

"I'm afraid so. Mrs. Williams's condition is deteriorating rather quickly. We've moved her out of the Alzheimer's unit and into the acute-care area, where we can watch her more closely. I thought you'd want to know."

"Yes," Shelly said, feeling ashamed of herself for not getting there to visit sooner, and now she had a cab waiting and a plane that wouldn't wait for her.

"Is she—are you telling me she's dying?" Shelly asked.

"I'm not sure," Mrs. Thompson said. "A woman with her condition could live a long time, but she's definitely taken a turn for the worse."

"Oh." Shelly sat down on the bar stool. Marion Williams could be dying, and she was all alone in the world. Shelly couldn't stand that idea. "Could I see her?"

"Of course."

She looked at her watch, heard the cab driver toot his horn again and thought of the plane she'd promised to be on.

It wouldn't take that long to go visit Marion. She'd just have to be on the next plane, she decided. Brian would have to understand. Shelly promised the woman she'd be there in a few minutes, then hung up the phone.

A quick call to the airport, and she'd switched her flight to one that left two hours later. Then she grabbed her stuff and left.

Shelly walked briskly down the hallway with the nurse she'd spoken with a few minutes before. "What do you think is wrong with her?" she asked. "I thought it might be years before she died."

"Alzheimer's is normally a disease that progresses slowly," the woman said. "But she's been very agitated since her husband's death. We've had trouble keeping her calm. We've tried to explain things to her as best we can. I think we finally succeeded."

"Oh," Shelly said. "You think this is a reaction to Charlie's death?"

"Either that or—I know it sounds hard to believe, but I've seen it before—she's simply given up. It may be that she doesn't want to go on anymore without her husband. The will to live is a very powerful thing, and losing it can have drastic physical consequences."

After seeing Marion Williams, Shelly did believe that the woman wanted to die. The nurses who had cared for her day in and day out told Shelly it might be a blessing if she did.

The woman wasn't going to get better, and her death could still be years away, the process one of a slow, agonizing deterioration of her body to match what had already happened to her mind. She had already suffered a great deal, and she might continue to do so for a long time to come.

"I'm sorry," Mrs. Thompson told her after she came out of Marion's room. "I know this is difficult."

Shelly nodded. "Is there anything we can do for her?"

"We'll do all we can. Her doctor was here this morning, and he thinks that right now it's going to be a waiting game. She might pull out of this. She might not."

"I'm glad you called me," Shelly said as they walked down the hall together.

"If it helps, I think she reached the point a long time ago where Mr. Williams would have been happy to see her pass away. He knew that she'd suffered more than anyone should have to. And if you believe there's a next life awaiting us, a better one, she deserves it. And she'd want to be with him."

"Yes, Charlie would want her with him, too," Shelly said, certain of that.

"Oh, there's one more thing," the nurse said. "We've gathered up Mrs. Williams's personal things from her room and put them into storage temporarily. I'm sure she'll want

her own things around her if she can come back to this wing.
But there was something there for you.''

''For me?''

''A big envelope with your name on it.''

Shelly didn't catch part of what the woman said. She was
so caught off guard that she just stood there, staring at the
envelope in the woman's outstretched hands.

Yes, that was her name, written in Charlie's handwrit-
ing. She finally managed to take the fat envelope with a
trembling hand.

''I need . . . Would you excuse me for a moment? I want
to look at this.''

''Of course,'' the woman said.

In a daze, Shelly walked to the end of the hall and sat
down on one of the benches in the hallway.

She turned the envelope over in her hand, opening the
flap, then pulling out the thick wad of papers—soil and
water analyses for a couple of construction projects the firm
was involved in. She checked the date—from a few months
before Grant left the firm, and he'd been the project manager on these jobs.

The first report was done by a subcontractor the firm had
hired in Miami to test for possible contamination at a condominium site across town. No, now that she looked more
closely, it was two sets of the same reports, one showing that
the site was fine as far as EPA standards were concerned and
the other showing some definite problems in both the soil
and the water.

She looked over the reports more closely—they were expensive problems to fix—involving work that could easily
run a half million dollars or more.

So this is what Grant had done—seen a problem with the
samples and made a duplicate report showing everything

was fine—then turned that report over to Williams Engineering's client.

Shelly felt sick as she shoved the reports back into the envelope and walked down the hall. She had what she needed. Grant had been falsifying reports, and Charlie must have found out about it. Grant had killed him for it.

Shelly turned the corner and headed for the pay phone at the end of the hall.

And she didn't even notice the man who was following her.

Chapter 18

Brian spent the morning in a battle with himself, trying to keep his mind on his work and the problems that had to be solved. He'd run through the entire mess, again and again, sure he'd missed something that was right under his nose.

But what?

"Mr. Sandelle? Do you know what time Shelly's coming in?" Maureen asked.

Brian pulled his head out of the papers in front of him long enough to answer. "She's not," he said, hoping he wouldn't have to explain too much. He didn't want anyone to know where she was. "She had some business to take care of, and she left town for a few days. If there's anything on her desk that needs to be taken care of right away, you can bring it to me."

"Oh, dear," the woman said. "Do you know if the nursing home got in touch with her before she left?"

"What?" he said, only half paying attention to the woman.

"Someone from the nursing home called this morning for her. There's some sort of problem with Marion, and they were trying to get hold of Shelly. I gave them your home number."

Maureen had been worried about Shelly after the break-in at her apartment, and Brian had told her that Shelly would be staying at his place. He was sure the secretary didn't think a thing of giving the number to the nursing home.

But it left Brian feeling a little uneasy.

"What time was this?" he asked. "When you gave them the number."

"A little after nine."

A little? It was the kind of description that left an engineer baffled. Time was measured in minutes and in seconds, not vague quantities like "a little." He needed to know the earliest time the call would have come to his house.

He'd left there, reluctantly, at 9:02. He'd wanted to put her on the plane himself, but he had to meet that lawyer.

She must have gotten on that plane, he told himself. He'd begged and bullied her until she'd promised to go. So she wouldn't have been there to take the call from the nursing home.

She was safe and sound, headed for Tallahassee.

"Maureen," he said, trying to keep his voice calm and even. "I bought a plane ticket in Shelly's name for a flight leaving this morning at nine-thirty. Would you call the airline for me, please, and see if she picked up the ticket?"

"Of course." The woman headed for the door

"Come and get me as soon as you find out," he called after her.

He got up, shut the office door, then blanked out on the name of Marion's nursing home. He flipped through the yellow pages. Nursing homes—he scanned the listings under that heading, then the display ads beside them.

There it was. He found the one where Marion stayed. He dialed the number, and as he waited impatiently for the call to go through, he looked over those ads again. They promised privacy, seclusion, a room that's not a room, one that will be a home away from home.

Home, he thought. The place had been Marion's home for years.

A home away from home—he didn't see how he could have overlooked that.

It was the only place they hadn't searched for whatever Grant Edwards wanted so desperately, and one of the few places Grant hadn't searched, as well.

He wondered if Grant Edwards realized that. He wondered if Grant could be there right now.

"Mr. Sandelle?" Maureen said. "Shelly never picked up the ticket."

He turned his head to the side and swore silently.

"But she did phone and change her reservation to a later flight, one that will leave—" the woman consulted her watch "—in just a few minutes. But she hasn't checked in yet."

And then Brian knew. He felt it like a knife in the gut.

That's where the records were.

That's where Shelly was.

He prayed that Grant Edwards wasn't there already, as well, even as he grabbed his keys and headed for the door.

Shelly shouldn't have been surprised to find herself face-to-face with Grant again. After all, she had what he was so desperately looking for; it was right here in her hand.

Unfortunately he did surprise her.

She didn't even see it coming, and she hadn't had time to tell anyone about what she'd found.

As she was making her way to the phone to make the call, she heard footsteps coming up behind her. Before she could get out of the way to let the person pass her, an arm reached out and grabbed her from behind, pulling her into one of the patient's rooms.

He threw her against the wall, then stood there in front of her, nervously tapping his foot on the tile floor while his eyes darted all around the room. "Hello, Shelly," he said finally, his voice shaking like a man who'd just run a two-minute mile.

"Grant," she said, searching the room herself. There were personal items scattered all around it, and the bed had clearly been slept in, though it was empty now.

The patient might be coming back anytime. Or one of the nurses might come. Anything to distract the man, to draw his attention away long enough for her to do something.

She could do it, she told herself. She could get away from him.

And that's when Grant pulled out a gun. She watched as he took the small revolver from his jacket pocket, flicked a switch with his thumb, then aimed it right at her.

"I know how to use this," he said, the sweat beading on the strip of skin above his top lip. "That sound was the safety coming off. I kept it on last time, because I really didn't want to hurt you."

Shelly looked around her for something she could grab, something she could use against him, but saw nothing. He had her with her back against the wall, literally.

"I didn't want to hurt anyone, Shelly. You've got to believe me. I didn't mean for any of this to happen."

"I..." She had to pause long enough to take a breath. "I'd like to think that you didn't, Grant."

"I didn't. That thing with Charlie...I never meant for that to happen. I swear it."

"All right," she said, ready to tell the man anything at this point. "What happened, Grant? What went wrong?"

"I just...I got into some trouble, with the horses. I hit a dry spell where I couldn't have picked my grandma out of a crowd, much less a good horse."

He was close enough now that Shelly could smell the alcohol on his breath. He'd been drinking—it wasn't even eleven o'clock in the morning. The hand that held the gun on her wasn't steady at all.

"I owed some people money," he said. "Lots of money. Bad people."

Shelly nodded, seeing again the records he'd altered. "So you did them a favor."

"Exactly," he said. "That's all it was. A little favor. Is that so bad?"

"No," she said, trying to soothe him.

"Exactly. I lost a little more money, did these guys a few more favors. Everything would have been fine. I was getting myself out of it, I swear. Then Charlie caught on to what I was doing."

"And he didn't like it?"

"No, but I knew he was in bad shape himself. He needed the money to keep his wife in this place. So he looked the other way for a while, and I passed a little of the money on to him."

Shelly had to look the other way herself then. She was so damned mad at them both. She'd had no idea Charlie was so desperate and that Grant had such a gambling problem.

"Then Charlie wanted out," Grant said, waving the gun along with his hands as he talked. "And once you're in, it's hard to get out. Next thing I knew, he fired me. I couldn't believe it. I didn't know what to do. I thought I'd just go to work somewhere else, then I could keep doing what I needed to do to get the money."

"I thought you went to work in Miami."

"I did, but ... I've been drinking a little lately," he said.

Shelly was surprised that he would admit it. Maybe he wasn't as far gone as she thought. "So what did you do then?"

"Decided I had to get Charlie to take me back. He wouldn't do it. He said he had records, proof of what I'd done, and he told me if I didn't leave him alone he'd turn me in.

"I couldn't let him do that. All I wanted to do was scare him into letting me come back to work. That's all. That thing with the plane—all I wanted to do was scare him a little. Get him to take me back. I never meant for it to crash, and I never thought you might be on it when it happened."

One more mystery solved, she thought. This man was insane.

"I like you, Shelly," he said in all sincerity, the gun still pointed at her. "I didn't want you to get hurt in any of this. That's why I called you, to warn you."

"Look," Shelly said. "It's not too late. If Charlie's death was an accident, the way you say it was, you can explain that to everyone. I'll help you, Grant. We'll make them understand."

"No." He shook his head. "It won't work."

"It might," she tried to reason with him. "What else are you going to do?"

"I don't know," he said, sweating and shaking.

Shelly thought she might be getting somewhere with him. Then the nurse walked in.

"Ahh!" The woman screamed, dropping the patient chart with its heavy metal casing to the floor.

It clattered, the sound echoing around the little room, startling Grant and giving the nurse a chance to escape back out the door.

Shelly heard her running and yelling for help as she went. She stayed there, frozen to the spot, with Grant between her and the door, wondering if she'd just blown her best chance of escape.

The nurse would call the police, she told herself. They would be here in minutes, and they'd get her out of here, if she didn't find a way out by herself first.

Grant liked her. He didn't want to hurt her. She believed he was telling her the truth about that, in his own twisted way. Of course, intent wasn't the most important thing here. He hadn't intended to hurt Charlie, either.

And Charlie was dead.

Brian sped up U.S. 41 toward the northeast side of town, and he called the nursing home while he drove. He was on hold at the moment, waiting for the nursing supervisor who'd tried to call Shelly this morning.

Grant Edwards was there. Shelly was there, too. He knew it as clearly as he'd known he had to get her out of Naples this morning.

The nursing supervisor finally picked up the phone. She had seen Shelly just a few minutes ago, but she'd lost track of her somewhere. She explained about the problem with Marion Williams, and Brian knew he was on to something when the woman told him about clearing out Marion's room.

The woman was just answering his questions about what she'd found when he heard the commotion of a woman screaming as she ran down the hallway.

A gun—he made that out clearly. A man with a gun down the hallway.

And he knew.

Shelly was there. Grant was there, and the man had another gun.

Brian wondered if Grant had the guts or the sheer stupidity to use it this time. He wondered whose head it was pointed at right then and whether the safety catch was on or off at that moment.

And as he pushed his foot down hard on the accelerator, he dialed the emergency dispatch office and promised himself that he wasn't going to lose her now.

Grant was growing more agitated with the sound of the sirens. "This is all I needed," he told Shelly, holding up the envelope. "Just this. And I've got it now."

"Well, maybe you should go now, Grant."

"Yeah." He wiped the sweat from his brow with the sleeve of his shirt. "Yeah, I should go."

"Grant, the police are coming. They're going to be here any minute. If you're going to leave, you need to go now."

He was pacing, from the window to the door and back again. "I don't know," he said. "It all got so complicated, you know?"

Shelly nodded. He seemed incredibly like a child at that moment.

"I didn't mean for any of this to happen."

"I know." She eased toward the door once again as he walked to the window. She wasn't that far from the door, but it opened inward. If only it opened the other way, she'd have a chance to get through it before he could react.

The sirens were roaring now, right outside the window.

"It's not too late," she said. "They're in front. You could go out the side entrance, but you have to hurry, Grant."

"I don't know," he said, staring at her. "What am I going to do with you? You know what's in here. You know what I did." He pointed the gun right at her. "You're going to have to come with me."

"I won't tell anyone," she said. "I promise."

Grant laughed, and the sound sent chills up her spine. "You won't tell?"

"That's right," she said. "I . . . I like you, Grant. I don't want to see you end up in jail."

"I can't go to jail," he said. "It was a mistake. That's all. And I can't go to jail. You can't let them send me to jail."

"I won't."

But he didn't believe her.

"You'll have to come with me."

He grabbed her by the arm and pulled her against him. He anchored her in front of him as a shield, holding her there with an arm around her chest, the gun to her head.

"Let's go."

The hallway in front of the door was deserted. But as they turned to go down the hallway, someone stepped in front of them.

Shelly wasn't sure who it was at first. There was a big, wide window at the end of the hall, the light coming through it almost blinding.

Grant stiffened behind her, then halted when the man didn't move.

He was right in the middle of the hallway, his empty hands hanging down to his sides. No weapon, no nothing, just one man between her and this madman and the door.

Oh, God, it was Brian.

"You're not going anywhere with her," he told Grant.

And then he just stood there in the middle of the hallway, as if sheer force was any match for a man with a gun. It was the most foolish thing she'd ever seen Brian Sandelle do, and the man was no fool.

For a minute, Shelly was sure he was up to something, some trick or something. But the seconds ticked by, the sound of running feet—the police no doubt—kept coming closer, and Brian just stood there.

Slowly, she came to realize that he didn't have any sort of plan, and he definitely didn't have any weapon. What did the man think he was going to do? Get himself killed, too?

"Get out of my way, man," Grant said nervously. He managed to keep the gun fairly steady now and pointed at her.

Brian just shook his head and stood his ground.

He'd lost his mind, Shelly thought. Both of them had, and she was the only sane person in this hallway.

"Get out of here." She mouthed the words to Brian.

But he wasn't budging.

"Grant," she said, wondering if the man with the gun could be any easier to talk to. "You have to go now...."

But the next thing she knew, it was too late. There was a clatter of running feet, tense, shouted orders to take cover because they'd spotted the man with the gun.

She heard one of the officers calling to Grant to let her go and throw down his gun unless he wanted to get hurt.

Shelly could feel the fear in the man who held her fiercely to him; it was almost as strong as her own panic. It seemed to swirl in the air around them, its power holding them in a paralyzing grip.

"Turn around, Grant," she told him, feeling the indecision in him.

"I don't know," he said. "I just... I don't know what to do."

"Turn around," she said softly, echoing the officer's impatient command.

Brian was still there in front of her, no more than a few feet away at that point, but she couldn't let herself look at him.

Why didn't he get out of the way?

And she couldn't help but think of that morning and the things he'd told her he wanted. Just a little time for the two of them, he'd said. Surely they deserved that and more. The one night, as wonderful as it had been, hadn't been nearly enough.

"Drop the gun, Mr. Edwards," one of the policemen said. "And let the woman go. This is your last chance."

"Do it, Grant. Do what the man says."

"I never wanted to hurt you," he said to Shelly, even as he cocked the gun. She watched as the gun that had been pointing more toward the ceiling than at her came down slowly toward her face.

"Get away from me," he yelled over his shoulder, then turned to her. "I'm sorry," he said, shifting beside her, bringing the gun around toward her—

A harsh cracking sound shot down the hallway. She thought at first Grant had pulled the trigger and wondered why she hadn't felt anything. Surely the gun was close enough to blow off the side of her face. But it didn't hurt, not in her face, at least. Grant's arm tightened around her in a punishing grip, and he moaned.

In the next instant, she felt something slam into her from the front and knock her to the floor as the second shot rang out.

Shelly hit hard against the floor, the breath knocked out of her, the solid weight of a man falling heavily on top of her.

Another shot rang out. Another body hit the floor.

Then it was all over.

* * *

Brian waited until the police ran past him and had Grant surrounded before he rolled off Shelly and turned her over, running his eyes up and down her body, looking for any sign that she'd been hurt. He wasn't sure he'd gotten to her in time, and he wasn't sure how good a shot the officer with the rifle was.

If he'd seen a drop of blood on her, he would have lost it right then and there.

Thankfully there was none.

"You all right?" he asked when he could trust himself to speak.

She nodded, breathing hard, her lower lip trembling. Hell, her whole body was trembling.

Brian found himself afraid to even touch her, to see that she was real and safe, sitting on the floor in front of him. He brushed off the officer's questions, not willing to let anyone pull his attention away from her in that moment, not willing to let anyone get between them.

Finally he reached out a hand to trace the only sign he could find that she'd been hurt—the reddened spot on her left cheekbone. "You're going to have another bruise, sweetheart."

And he'd put this one on her himself when he'd knocked her to the floor.

She nodded, then looked out of the corner of her eye to the commotion to the left of them.

Brian saw the blood pooling on the floor. The police were holding Grant down, and a couple of the nurses were working over him now.

It could have been Shelly. He tried not to even think it, but he couldn't help himself. A few inches to the right, a slightly unsteady hand, an officer who'd hesitated a moment too long—any one of those things and it could so easily have been her on the floor in a pool of blood, rather than Grant Edwards.

He'd come so close to losing her.

"Oh, God," Shelly said, turning away from the sight of the man sprawled out on the floor.

And then whatever had been holding him back, whatever had made him hesitate to touch her again, gave way. He hauled her into his arms, and he didn't let go for a long, long time.

Chapter 19

The next thirty hours were insane. Police questions, EPA officials' questions, city building code enforcers' questions, press questions, employees' questions.

Grant Edwards, up to his ears in debt because of his poor ability to pick a winning horse, had been terrified of his debt to some tough-talking loan shark.

He'd been desperate enough, stupid enough and scared enough to do all this, when the whole time he'd been in debt to some two-bit bookie who happened to talk a good game of intimidation in an effort to get his money.

Grant Edwards had simply panicked and caused all this chaos. Once he got out of the hospital, he was going to pay for it by going to jail.

Meanwhile, Brian was going to see what he could do about saving the business Charlie had spent his life building, so he might be able to repay the man's debts and keep his wife comfortable for the last few weeks or months of her life.

It didn't look good for the firm or for Marion Williams. Brian had hardly had time to breathe, much less figure out how to save the business, especially with the EPA, the city building inspection people and the professional licensing board coming down on it all at the same time.

And he didn't want to be doing any of that, anyway. He wanted to make Shelly tell him what was bothering her.

He thought for a while that she was simply mad at him over that nasty scene they'd had at the nursing home once he'd convinced himself she was safe and sound. He'd handled it badly. How many times had he admitted to something like that in the past two weeks? He shook his head in disgust.

He'd actually yelled at her back there at the nursing home. He'd demanded to know why the hell she hadn't gotten herself on that plane to Tallahassee the way she'd promised him she would. And then she'd yelled right back, telling him that stepping in between Grant Edwards, his gun and the door had been the stupidest thing he'd ever done.

He could have explained that quite easily, but she hadn't wanted to listen. She'd stormed away, and he'd let her go.

Obviously he hadn't been thinking as clearly as he should have. Hell, who was he kidding, he hadn't been thinking straight in a while now, and it was all her fault. The woman had damned near scared him to death, and he'd lost his temper with her again.

He glanced at the clock on the wall as he walked through the nearly deserted office. He could see her standing in the hallway, staring at one of the site plans tacked up onto the wall.

She'd spent the night at her own apartment, when he'd wanted her back in his bed at his house.

The woman who'd been so soft and yielding in his arms for a few precious moments after Grant had been shot—she was nowhere to be found yesterday afternoon or today. She'd been downright cool toward him, as if she hadn't turned to fire in his arms two nights ago.

He wondered if she regretted that now, and he thought he might know why. He thought she might believe, mistakenly, that it hadn't meant nearly as much to him as it did to her, and he figured it was time to set the woman straight.

He was on his way to do that when Maureen looked up from her desk and called out to him.

"Mr. Sandelle? Phone for you. And if it's all right, I think I'll be going now."

"Sure, go ahead," he said, heading back to his office to pick up the call.

He was only half paying attention to the call—some engineering firm in San Francisco checking a reference for someone who was job hunting—when he realized it was Shelly.

The guy was talking about Shelly. Hell, he was ready to hire her and put her to work in a couple of weeks.

Brian was furious all over again. It was all he could do not to tell the guy that she wasn't going anywhere anytime soon.

In the end, he wasn't sure exactly what he'd told the man. He just knew that he managed to get off the phone so he could make sure she hadn't left the office yet.

He found her still standing in front of the site plan. There were a couple of people in the office, he reminded himself, and managed to ask her quite calmly to step into his office. He had to remind himself not to lose his temper, the way he had the day before. It would only make things more difficult.

It made him furious when she tried to pretend that there was nothing between them and that he had no right to try to protect her. He couldn't stop that particular feeling, any more than he could clamp down on any of the others he had for her.

He'd been protective of her from the time she was six, when she had been one of the loneliest, saddest, sweetest kids he'd ever met. The feeling was so deeply ingrained in him, he wouldn't ever be able to pry it out of himself—just as he was sure all the other feelings he had for her would be with him forever, as well.

He was just surprised it had taken him so long to figure it all out.

"Is something wrong?" she asked finally, drawing him back to the situation at hand.

"A misunderstanding, I'm sure," he said. "There's a man in San Francisco who's under the impression that you want to come to work for him."

"Yes."

"You can't go," he said, praying for some self-control here.

"Why not?"

"Because you can't leave me now."

"Oh, Brian."

He'd gotten her all flustered, at least—not the reaction for which he was hoping, but better than nothing.

"What?" He prodded her.

"I've stayed too long already," she said. "I'll clear up everything I can with Marion, but her doctor doesn't think she's going to survive much longer. And I'll help you as much as I can with the office stuff, but after that . . ."

"What about us?" he asked.

"What about us?" she said, as if she had no idea what he meant. "I'm in love with you. I always have been—"

"And that's reason to leave?"

Shelly leaned back in her chair, trying to put some distance between them. She hadn't expected this to be easy, but she hadn't expected him to make it so hard for her, either.

The man had called from San Francisco yesterday, and she'd known this job was her chance to get away from Brian while she still could. If she stayed, it would only get harder to leave in the end.

Of course, it was damned near impossible as it was.

"Don't make me say this," she begged him.

"Say what? I don't get it. I don't know what the problem is. How could you want to leave now that we've—"

"Now that we've what? Figured out that we're good in bed together?"

"Is that all it was?" he challenged her.

"Not for me, but what about you?"

He seemed quite taken aback by that, and if she hadn't known better, she would have sworn she'd hurt him then. She'd clearly surprised him, though she didn't see why. Unless he simply hadn't expected her to be so up-front about this whole thing.

"Look," she said, striving for calm when she felt anything but that. "I've spent years with all these feelings, years when I've done nothing but compare myself to Rebecca and wish I could become her—for you. But I can't."

"I don't want you to be Rebecca. I want you to be you."

"All right." She took a deep breath and tried again. "I can't let myself settle for being the woman you're with because you can't have Rebecca."

"First," he said, ticking off his points. "Rebecca is married. She's out of my life, and I'm not looking for a substitute for her.

"Next—are you trying to tell me that there's still some doubt in your mind about how much I want you?"

He had at least three more points he intended to go over with her, but the disbelief in her eyes about his last statement was more than he could handle in a civilized fashion.

She'd already accused him of being practically barbaric a few days ago, so he figured he didn't have anything to lose by giving in to a few more of those feelings.

He hauled her up out of the seat so she was standing in front of him, his eyes boring down into her. "Do you honestly think I make a habit of making love to women on my bathroom countertop? Or on the floor? Because I'm so damned desperate to have them I can't make it the five feet to the bed?"

She couldn't help but blush at that. It had been a long time before they'd made it to the bed. And she was certain that no man had ever been so passionately intent on pleasing her.

But that didn't make it love.

She picked her words very carefully. "I know you have some sort of desire for me."

He scoffed at that, laughing sarcastically. "Some sort of desire?"

He seemed to be rather insulted by that. He got up, walked to the door and locked it, then pulled off his suit coat and threw it across the back of the other chair.

"We don't have to argue about this. I can show you this 'some sort of desire' I have for you."

He pushed the papers aside from the front edge of his desk. They fell in a heap to the floor, but he didn't seem to care. He was loosening his tie.

Shelly felt the color rise in her cheeks, felt the blood heating within her veins. And she felt the first real stirrings of uneasiness inside her as the situation spiraled into something so completely out of her control.

"I know what desire feels like," she told him desperately. "Believe it or not, over the course of my life, there have been men who've desired me."

"Not like I have," he said through clenched jaws. "And I have no trouble believing that other men have wanted you, although I could do without being reminded of them."

Shelly didn't know what to say then. She didn't know what to do. He was positively seething mad, and that wasn't like him.

She put a hand up to hold him off when he would have come closer, but that was a mistake. He'd gotten his tie loose, but not the buttons of his shirt. The white cotton was still between them, but it didn't matter. She could feel the heat coming off him, and she could feel every beat of his heart.

"Oh, hell," she said, pulling her hand away.

She would have turned away, as well, but his arms came up to hold her there, less than a foot away. And he wasn't going to let go.

Shelly accepted that and dropped her eyes, at least. "Regardless of what it *was* . . . It wasn't what I want. It wasn't what I need. It wasn't *love.*"

"Wasn't it?" He dared her to deny it.

"You damned well know it wasn't. You don't love me," she said. "And damn you for making me say it for you."

"Shelly, what do you think I was doing yesterday when I stepped into that hallway?"

She didn't even want to think about it.

"I knew he had you, and I didn't think the police were going to get there in time," Brian said. "I knew he had a gun, too, and I didn't care. Because there was no way I was going to let him walk out of that building with you."

His hands tightened on her arms for just a moment before he let her go. He didn't say a word for the longest time.

He just watched her as she stood there in front of him, try-ing to make sense of it all.

Except, she couldn't. It didn't make any sense to her. He wasn't a stupid man, and he'd taken an incredible risk yes-terday, for her.

Sometime in the night she'd spent without him, she de-cided she couldn't let herself settle for less. "I need for someone to love me," she said, tired of dancing around the whole thing. "I deserve it."

He nodded, and she thought she was finally getting through to him.

"I'm not going to settle for less," she vowed. "I thought maybe I could. I tried to talk myself into it last night, be-cause I want so much to be with you. But I can't settle for that. And you can't tell me you love me."

He understood then. She saw the knowledge settle upon him, calming him as nothing else could have.

"No," he admitted. "I don't think I can."

Shelly did manage to move away from him then. She backed up to the window and turned to the side, shaking in earnest now. She stared at the floor, then the ceiling, then out the window, when all she really wanted to do was bury her face in her hands.

It shouldn't hurt to hear it like that. She'd known it was true all along. It wasn't as if she'd wanted him to lie about his feelings, just so she could hear the words from him. But it hurt so much to hear them.

This was going to kill her, she decided. Loving this man was going to rip her soul to shreds. It was happening right now.

And he was watching the whole thing.

It took all she had in her, every bit of her shaken pride and determination, to stand up straight and look him right in the eye. She'd expected to see pity there. It burned in her gut—

the idea of looking up at him and seeing the pity for her in his eyes. She'd expected the guilt, too, about the night they'd spent together, even when she'd gone more than willingly to his bed.

But this look in his eyes—it didn't look like pity. It didn't look like guilt.

He looked quite pleased with himself, something she couldn't understand, even as he reached out his arms to her and hauled her up against him.

Her hands landed flush against his chest, once again trying to hold some distance between them and succeeding only marginally. She could feel his heart racing along, strong and fast, inside his chest. She could feel the fine trembling in him, the one that matched the trembling in her.

His eyes were dark and dangerous and smoky looking, the way they'd been the night before in his steamy bathroom. He was watching her lips intently. She could imagine what his would feel like on hers, and she knew he was imagining that, as well.

"What?" She had to struggle to find her voice. "What in the world is going on?"

He smiled, beautifully, a little mischievously, and it left her dumbfounded.

"Brian?"

"I don't think I can tell you that I love you—" he took her face in his hands, refusing to let her look anywhere else but at him, and he was still smiling "—because I don't think you'd believe me right now.

"Everything's happened so fast, Shel. It's all been so crazy, and it's only been a few days. I'd gladly say the words if I thought it would do any good, but I don't. You'd only doubt me and try to tell me I didn't know what I was feeling, although I'm certain that I do."

Dumbstruck, she said nothing, just opened her mouth to his when it came down for a quick, hard kiss.

"Now as I see it," he said, "there's only one thing left to do."

She simply couldn't speak. He was waiting for her to ask him what there could possibly be left to do, but she couldn't say a word.

He just smiled and continued. "We'll have to figure out some way I can convince you that I love you."

Shelly swayed on her feet, and she thought for a minute she was going to have heart failure. She felt this tremendous weight in her chest, felt her heart swell to the point of bursting, then it all came loose and she finally dared to believe. This all-encompassing joy flooded through her entire body, this warm, tingling sensation that she thought must feel something like being reborn.

Every dream she'd ever had had just come true.

"Tell me again," she said.

He shook his head back and forth, hauling her up against him when her legs gave out. "Just give me some time. I'm going to show you. I'll find a million ways to make you believe it."

*   *   *   *   *

Another wonderful year of romance
concludes with

Christmas
Memories

Share in the magic and memories of romance
during the holiday season with this collection of two
full-length contemporary Christmas stories,
by two bestselling authors

Diana Palmer
Marilyn Pappano

Available in December at your favorite retail outlet.

Only from

Silhouette®

™

where passion lives.

ETERNAL LOVE
by Maggie Shayne

Fans of Maggie Shayne's bestselling Wings in the Night miniseries have heard the whispers about the one known as Damien. And now the most feared and revered of his kind has his own story in TWILIGHT ILLUSIONS (SS #47), the latest in this darkly romantic, sensual series.

As he risks everything for a mortal woman, characters from the previous books risk their very existence to help. For they know the secrets of eternal life—and the hunger for eternal love....

Don't miss TWILIGHT ILLUSIONS by Maggie Shayne, available in January, only from Silhouette Shadows

Return to the classic plot lines you love, with

January 1995 rings in a new year of the ROMANTIC TRADITIONS you've come to cherish. And we've resolved to bring you more unforgettable stories by some of your favorite authors, beginning with Beverly Barton's THE OUTCAST, IM #614, featuring one very breathtaking bad boy!

Convict Reese Landry was running from the law— and the demons that tortured his soul. Psychic Elizabeth Mallory knew he was innocent...and in desperate need of the right woman's love.

ROMANTIC TRADITIONS continues in April 1995 with Patricia Coughlin's LOVE IN THE FIRST DEGREE, a must-read innovation on the "wrongly convicted" plot line. So start your new year off the romantic way with ROMANTIC TRADITIONS—only in

And now for something completely different....

SPELLBOUND
ROMANCE

In January, look for
SAM'S WORLD (IM #615)
by Ann Williams

Contemporary Woman: Marina Ross had
landed in the strangest of worlds: the future.
And her only ally was the man responsible for
bringing her there.

Future Man: Sam's world was one without
emotion or passion, one he was desperately
trying to save—even as he himself felt the first
stirrings of desire....

Don't miss SAM'S WORLD,
by Ann Williams, available this January,
only from

INTIMATE MOMENTS®
Silhouette®

SPELL6

Southern
Knights

by Marilyn Pappano

Award-winning author Marilyn Pappano's
Southern Knights series continues in
December 1994 with REGARDING REMY, IM #609.

Wounded Special Agent Remy Sinclair needed
some down-home TLC, and nurse Susannah Duncan
seemed like the perfect candidate. Almost *too*
perfect. And before long, Remy had to wonder if
his tantalizing angel of mercy had come to help—
or harm.

And don't miss A MAN LIKE SMITH, featuring Assistant
U.S. Attorney Smith Kendricks. His story is coming your
way in April 1995.

So immerse yourself once again in the Southern style
of living and loving, as three men bound by honor
and friendship find the women of their dreams,
only in...

INTIMATE MOMENTS®
Silhouette®